PARADISE CAFÉ

PARADISE CAFÉ

STELLA KALB

PALMETTO
PUBLISHING
Charleston, SC
www.PalmettoPublishing.com

Paradise Café
Copyright © 2023 by Stella Kalb

First Edition

Paperback ISBN: 979-8-8229-2647-9

To my friends and family:
My thanks and gratitude go out to you.

PROLOGUE

It was the life people dreamed of but were never able to fulfill for fear of relocation and expensive living. Santa Barbara, a sleepy college town for the elite and most studious of individuals. A town of current wealth and old money; a town high above the rest. The smell of sea salt and the vision of palm trees along the ocean roads coincided with pine trees just a few yards away at the base of whispering hills. Tourists visit every weekend and students work locally to pay their massive rent and tuition. Most are privileged and don't need to bother. Outside cafés and shops line the main strip in the middle of town. The bell of a streetcar captures the attention of passersby. The jazz club in the middle of town is for members only and requires a dress code. Built for dreamers and lovers, the bartender pours a concoction in a hurricane glass and slides it across the bar for the waiter to catch at The Paradise Café.

CHAPTER 1

Music filled Samantha's living room with the sliding glass door open to the terrace overlooking the Pacific Ocean. Coffee was brewing while she checked her e-mail on her lap top this early morning. It was 6:30 am and she kept the music low so not to wake the neighbors. Her internal clock was off from the jet lag. Samantha's body was on East coast time for now. She had just spent the last ten days flying around the Eastern states picking up extra hours for her job at American Airlines. Samantha finally has five days off in a row to do nothing but relax in her Santa Barbara beach house. She has no roommates or pets although she loves animals but travels too much to care for one. She inherited this home from her deceased parents. Ever since she was five years old, she came here every summer with her family and couldn't part with it. The home was built in the 1960's and painted baby blue.

The front of the house faced the mountains and the back of the house faced the ocean. The homes on her street were close together and not very private. When she goes out on the terrace, she can have a conversation with her neighbor 4 yards away. Samantha turned off the David Bowie CD and took her coffee out to the terrace with her bathrobe wrapped tight to breathe in the salty air. She noticed her next-door neighbor Margaret on her terrace smoking a Newport cigarette.

"Good morning, Margaret. You're up early," said Samantha.

"Hey you. I didn't know you were back in town. Jack was asking about you last night," replied Margaret.

Margaret was in her early 50's, widowed, and had a raspy voice from years of smoking and partying. Her skin was prematurely aging from too much sun exposure and surfing back in her day. She hasn't touched a surf board since her husband was killed in a surfing accident 10 years ago. Now she's a pack-a-day smoker and drinks scotch at night.

"I got in early last night and went straight to bed. How is Jack?"

"The same womanizer he always is. You know Jack, always chasing tail," smiled Margaret as she blew smoke into the air.

Jack was the bartender at Paradise Café and made a mean martini. All of the well-to-do people in town knew who he was and he only slept with wealthy women. You needed a membership to visit Paradise Café Jazz Club which Samantha and Margaret had from years of living in the town and Samantha's father funded the project before he passed away. Only the elite met there for dinner, drinks, and business meetings. They even closed the club a couple of times for Bill Gates and his entourage. The club was known to hold small concerts for big name jazz musicians like Chris Botti, Rick Braun, and even Diana Krall played there once or twice. Famous people have homes a few miles away in Montecito. The Ritz Carlton Hotel stood over a cliff on the edge of town. Wealthy individuals occupied the hotel and rode limos to the club at night which sat in the middle of town. It was easy for Jack to get some action. He looked like a tan, male super-model. He worked-out and surfed all day and bartended at the club at night. Jack made good money in tips. He was a smooth talker and knew how to work the ladies.

"I spent the last couple of days in Key West...."

"Of course, you did," Margaret interrupted. "What's his name?"

"Come on, I don't have that many male interests. He's a sweet man and I don't know much about him. We only spoke for twenty minutes when we were changing planes in Miami. His name is Jay and he gave me his business card," said Samantha.

Margaret lit another cigarette. "So, you didn't get to sleep with him?"

"No, I don't even know him. He did slip a handsel into my hand-bag before I boarded the plane; something to remember him by."

"A picture of his penis?" Margaret laughed as Samantha giggled and almost choked on her coffee.

"Actually, it was a sand dollar he found in The Keys."

"It's rare to find one of those in Florida. So, is he legit? He's not married, gay, or a serial killer?"

"I have no idea. I'll have to check it out," replied Samantha.

"Are you going to the club tonight?" asked Margaret.

"I'm thinking about it. Are *you*? We can ride together."

"Ok. By then, you should have more news about lover boy," Margaret said as she took another puff of her cigarette.

"For sure. I better start the laundry and get my errands done. Do you want me to stop by around 7:30?"

"Sounds good, see you then."

Samantha went back in the house and put on an Elton John CD.

The sun was setting on the Pacific Ocean and the seagulls flew over the neighborhood. The time was 7:10 pm and Samantha looked through her closet for something to wear. She decided on a black pant suit with a pink sequins blouse. It was very classy, chic. She spritzed some Ralph Lauren perfume on her neck, put her hair in a clip, and put gloss over her red lipstick. She was ready to go and headed towards Margaret's house.

"Hey, you look amazing," said Margaret.

"So do you. Should I drive?"

Margaret had on a sundress with spaghetti straps that revealed her tan and wedge heels.

"Sure, you can drive. Let me grab my smokes." They both got into Samantha's sporty BMW and drove off. The club was only a few minutes away.

"So, did you do any research on your man? Is he clean?"

"He seems to be. I did call the restaurant where he works and he was there. We spoke for a few minutes and he e-mailed me."

"What if he's married?"

"He's not. I checked it out. He's been divorced for three years."

"How much did that cost you?"

"Fifty dollars," replied Samantha.

"I guess it's worth it. It's better than getting your heart broken. Let's hope he doesn't have women on the side."

"I'm sure he does. He's gorgeous you know."

The two of them arrived at the club and the valet attendant took their car and parked it. The doorman opened the door for them and Jack saw them right away. He came around the bar and greeted them with a kiss on the cheek.

"How are you beautiful ladies? Looking good, Sam." Jack winked.

"Thank you, Jack."

"You've been away for a few days, haven't you?"

"Almost two weeks. I leave again next week," replied Samantha.

"Are the two of you here for dinner or drinks?"

"Both. We're starving," replied Margaret.

"I'll show you to your table. Juan Compra will be playing tonight. I think he's your favorite, Sam."

"One of my favorites. We'll have our usual drinks please."

"I'll get right to it."

Margaret and Samantha were regulars at the club and everyone knew their name; even the musicians. The ladies had the menu memorized so there was no reason to look at it. Jack brought the drinks over with a complimentary appetizer.

"These potato skins look delicious! Thanks Jack," said Margaret.

"You're welcome, ladies. I'll be at the bar for a moment and then I'll be back to take your order."

"I can't wait to dive into a filet mignon steak. I've been craving one for a while," said Margaret.

"I think I'll stick to my usual Mahi."

Juan Compra entered through the back door and the guests started pouring in through the front.

"It looks like it will be busy in here tonight. It's a good thing we came in early. You mentioned you're leaving again next week. Where to?" asked Margaret.

"I'm working the West coast for four days and then Vegas for another four to visit with Melanie. I'm thinking of asking Jay to meet me there. What do you think?"

"It sounds like a good idea. You can get to know him and Vegas is the perfect place. It has beautiful women so you can see how he interacts with them. You know. . . make sure he's not a player. Where will you stay?"

"I usually stay with Melanie in that huge house of hers. Is that who I think it is?" said Samantha as she turned with a surprised look on her face.

A rock star walked through the back door wearing sunglasses and a red silk shirt. He was carrying a lap top bag strapped around his shoulder and a bottle of water in his left hand. He extended his right hand to Juan Compra, shook his hand and gave him a quick hug. He couldn't have been taller than 5'6". Jack arrived at the table to take the ladies' order.

"You ladies are in for a treat tonight. Look who's going to jam with Juan?"

"I can't believe it! Did you know about this Jack?" asked Samantha.

"There was a rumor but now it is justified. Juan's pianist had a family emergency so Billy is filling in for the night. He's been here before. They are good friends."

"Billy who?" asked Margaret.

"Billy Taylor, the rock star!" said Samantha with her eyes opened wide.

"Are you fuckin' serious?! That's it. We're staying the whole night. Keep the drinks coming Jack."

Jack took their order and went back to the bar. The place filled up fast and it was standing-room only. Everyone was dressed very nicely.

Samantha looked around the room smiling from ear to ear. Billy set up his lap top on top of the grand piano and took off his sunglasses. The crowd clapped and yelled in excitement. The 'Paradise Café' neon sign was lit on the back wall of the stage and Billy and Juan posed for a picture as Jack brought a drink for the both of them. Billy plugged in the microphones and tested the sound.

"Testing... one, two, three... testing. Testing one... I better use the facilities before we get started." Billy smiled and walked off the stage. The women squealed with delight. Juan spoke to the audience while Billy was away for a few minutes. He was wearing black leather pants and an amaranthine silk shirt. Billy came back and he announced his presence.

"It's great to be here in Santa Barbara! This was unexpected but I'm glad I am here to jam with my great friend, Juan Compra."

The audience clapped and squealed.

"We're going to keep things mellow tonight and keep the drinks coming Jack," said Billy as he started playing his guitar. They played for an hour and took a twenty-minute break. Billy and Juan sat down with Samantha and Margaret. The ladies were very surprised. Juan had met Samantha before and wanted to get to know her.

"You talented men must be hungry. Here, have some bread." Samantha handed Juan the bread basket.

"I remember you ladies from the last time I was here. You are Sam, and you are Margaret. This is my famous colleague, Billy," said Juan. Billy kissed the back of each lady's hand.

"Oh, a gentleman," said Samantha.

"But of course," said Billy. They talked some more before the boys went back on stage. They played for another hour and fifteen minutes. Juan finished the set with a trumpet solo.

"Thank you so very much for letting us play here tonight at Paradise Café. We love you! Good night," said Juan as he waved to the crowd. The audience clapped and hollered and came up to the stage for a complimentary CD. Billy went straight to the bar for his last drink.

"What's the story with the ladies? Are they single?" asked Billy as he smiled at the girls from a distance.

"They are single. Margaret is a little weathered. She smokes and drinks every day. Sam is a flight attendant and probably gets a lot of action but will never admit it."

Billy shook Jack's hand. "It was great meeting you. I might see you in a few months."

"I'll be here. Have a good night."

CHAPTER 2

Samantha turned off her cell phone and placed it in her carry-on luggage and boarded the plane. Her navy-blue pumps matched her uniform. She only had to stay one night in Seattle as she worked her way down the coast with many lay-overs and text messages from Jay. Samantha was looking forward to seeing Jay in Las Vegas. She spent two nights in San Francisco before heading to Vegas where she will meet her best friend Melanie that she hasn't seen in almost a year, since the funeral of Melanie's late husband. Melanie would spend her summers in Las Vegas as an exotic dancer to pay for law school that she never finished. An older, wealthy, gentleman swept her off her feet and she married three months later. To her inconvenience he passed away eleven months into the marriage from Cancer that he didn't know he had and left her millions.

Samantha noticed she was developing a cough before she landed in Vegas. She didn't know if it was from the dry cabin air or if she was catching a virus. Samantha didn't want to be sick on this trip. She stopped at a gift shop after landing to pick up cough drops.

The light pink limo pulled up to the curb and the license plate frame read 'Dance with Me'. Melanie rolled down the window.

"Hey Sugar! Get in."

The driver opened the trunk and put the luggage inside.

"I see you haven't changed much," said Samantha as she let out a cough.

"Oh honey, you need a shot of rum. Let me fix you up."

Michael Bublé played on the stereo and Melanie grabbed the top shelf rum from the limo bar and poured a shot.

"Don't worry. I'll join you. This is good stuff."

Melanie always called everyone 'Baby', 'Honey', or 'Sugar'. It was easier than remembering names. She learned this from her dancing days and never broke the habit. Melanie was always dolled-up with her re-constructed face and fake breasts. She always had a smile on her face and Samantha couldn't figure out if it was the booze, the Xanax, or the fact that she probably rolled around naked on top of cash every morning. Melanie was a bubbly brunette and everyone who met her wanted to get to know her. Vegas was the perfect town for her personality.

"I'm going to draw you a hot bath as soon as we get home. Are you hungry? I can order Chinese and we'll stay in until Jay gets here. Where's he staying?"

"He's staying at Bellagio and his flight doesn't get in until 10:30 pm."

"That gives us six hours to chill. Is he expecting you to stay with him?"

"Oh God, I hope not. I literally have only known him for a total of twenty minutes. I don't know him well at all. I'm sure he has many female companions."

"I wouldn't worry too much Sugar. You can get any man you want. We just need to take care of that cough of yours. By the way, how is Paradise Café?"

"Fabulous as usual."

"And Jack?"

"Always asking about you. You should come back with me. I have time off you know," suggested Samantha.

"I have a charity event Monday right after you leave. Maybe I can catch a flight in the late evening."

"That's a great idea. Let's plan on that. Margaret says hello."

"It'll be good to see the gang," said Melanie as she chugged the rest of her rum.

The ladies reached Melanie's home in the private community of her neighborhood. The security guard let the limo through and they reached the house and got out of the large vehicle. Samantha got settled into the large guest room with a glorious bathroom. Melanie made a bubble bath, lit the candles, and turned on soft music while Samantha unpacked.

"I love this huge closet. Look at all of the costume jewelry! I can live in here," said Samantha.

"Pick what you like. It's yours. Those are things I've collected through the years. I'm going to give most of it to charity anyway."

"I like these black pearls. It will go with my outfit tonight."

"I think I got those from AVON. See that shiny bracelet? That was a tip from a nice gentleman when I was dancing."

"You have all the luck."

"Not yet. I need a man to share my life with. I don't feel complete. A lot of men want to date me but it's hard to trust anyone. Do they like me or my money? Your bath is ready. I'll order the food. See you in a bit."

She gently closed the door and headed downstairs to the kitchen.

There was a message on Samantha's phone. Jay wanted to meet both of them for a midnight snack at Bellagio. He was looking forward to meeting Melanie and getting to know Samantha. Samantha relaxed in the tub for thirty minutes and drank half a bottle of sparkling water with half a dose of cough syrup. She was feeling quite better. She showered off, wrapped a towel around her head, and put a fluffy robe on and headed downstairs to eat.

"Jay wants to meet us at Bellagio around 11:30. Is that too late?"

"No, of course not. We'll take a nap right after we eat. It's 7:00 now. That will give us time. I'll phone the driver."

"Is he on call 24/7?"

"No. I have three drivers. They work 8-hour shifts even if I don't need them, they still get paid. Larry set it up that way. They get paid very well," Melanie explained.

Their families received lavish gifts at Christmas time plus a $5,000 bonus. Larry was Melanie's former husband that became a wealthy business man. He owned three hotel casinos. One of them was the Stardust which was a great success before closing down at the turn of the century.

The ladies arrived at Bellagio hotel and they immediately went to the nearest bar for Cosmopolitans. They took their drinks and strolled through the indoor garden and waited for Jay's call. Jay called from his suite and they decided to meet at the jazz lounge. He was near the entrance wearing black suede loafers, gray slacks, and a lavender silk dress shirt. He looked like he just walked out of GQ magazine with his five o'clock shadow. He smelled nice and had a lot of class. Jay kissed both ladies on the cheek and introduced himself to Melanie.

"I've heard so much about you, sugar," said Melanie.

"Ditto. The music is amazing here. I know the owner but he is in Europe right now. Let's have a seat. I see you ladies already have drinks."

"We took a stroll through the garden. Have you seen it?" asked Samantha.

"It's been a few years but tomorrow I will go."

The three of them got to know each other well. Melanie did most of the talking since this was her home town and she made them laugh.

It was 3:00 am and the musicians said 'good night' and started to put their instruments away.

"Where did the time go? We were just getting to know each other. Let's do lunch tomorrow," said Samantha.

"We can do that and the wax museum too if you're interested. I know the owner. I use to dance for him," said Melanie as they all laughed.

Jay walked the ladies to the car, kissed Samantha on the lips, and called it a night. As the driver drove off, Samantha rolled her window down and waved at Jay and stared until he was no longer visible.

"I haven't seen that look in a while, girlfriend. You've got him under your skin."

"That's a great song. Isn't it?" smiled Samantha.

Morning came and Samantha woke up to a wonderful text message from Jay. She texted back and went to the kitchen to make coffee. The aroma filled the kitchen with delight as Samantha ate yogurt and fruit.

She poured two cups and put them on a silver tray with cream and sugar and took it to Melanie's room and woke her up.

"Hey sleeping beauty. Here's your coffee; nice and strong."

"Oh my God. You're amazing. What time is it?"

"Eleven a.m."

"What time are we meeting Prince Charming?"

"Two thirty or three."

"I like him. He might be a keeper," smiled Melanie as she sipped her coffee.

"Do you want fruit or something?"

"You're the guest. I should be waiting on you."

"Don't be ridiculous."

"Hey, check out the woolgathering in the tree outside. I haven't seen doves like those in years. I'm going to open the window so we can hear them chirp and sing."

Melanie loved all animals and donated money to different animal charities. The girls enjoyed their coffee and then Samantha went upstairs to shower and get ready while Melanie made a few phone calls.

The clouds rolled in and it started to rain. Jay agreed to meet the girls at The Peppermill restaurant. Jay arrived first and waited a few minutes before seeing Melanie's limo pull up. The ladies were wearing jeans and boots and Jay wore the same but donned a NY Yankees jacket to complete the ensemble. He was a season ticket holder and knows a couple of the players. The hostess took Jay's name and they waited in the cocktail lounge which had a sunken fire place with a large circular sofa all the way around. There was a salt water aquarium to the left dividing the restaurant from the lounge.

"You smell nice Jay," said Samantha.

"You as well."

They sat down and Jay put Samantha's hand on his knee and he ordered a round of iced teas.

"So Jay, what is the name of your lovely restaurant in New York City?" asked Melanie.

"Logo's Bar & Grill. Here's my card. If you're ever in town you get a free dinner."

"I'll be sure and remember that." Melanie gave him a sexy smile and her eyes wandered over to a handsome man at the bar. The gentleman at the bar lifted his glass and winked at Melanie. Samantha noticed the two of them making eye contact and smiled at Melanie.

"Someone you know?"

"He looks familiar but I'm not sure who he is. Maybe a previous client."

"Have you dated much since Larry passed?"

"Not much. It's only been a year and a half."

"Honey, your purse is vibrating. It might be a text," said Jay.

The hostess called them into the restaurant. "Your table is ready. Would you like a wine list?"

"No thank you," answered Samantha as she walked and read her text message. "I'm sorry I answered for all of us. I just assumed it was too early for us to be drinking."

"That's ok. It probably is too early but I'm on New York time," said Jay jokingly.

Supertramp was playing on the stereo and they arrived at the table.

"I love classic rock. I haven't heard this in years," said Samantha.

"You love everything. You have a good ear for music," said Melanie as she looked at Jay. "You know, Sam loves everything from the 50's to present day. She knows her stuff."

"That's why I like her so much. She's artistic and worldly."

"Well, I do travel a lot. Are you going to talk to your friend at the bar?" asked Samantha.

"Probably not. He's not my type."

"What do you mean he's not your type? He's breathing."

The three of them laughed and Jay excused himself to use the restroom.

"So, girl, who's texting you? I saw you blush."

"It was Juan Compra. He played at Paradise Café two weeks ago. He wants to see me sometime."

"Lucky you. You have men all over the place. I mean that in a good way."

"You should call Jack sometime. He asked about you the last time I saw him."

"Isn't he a womanizer?"

"Yes, but he needs a strong woman to settle down with. Someone to keep him in line. You're strong and beautiful."

"Thanks Sam," said Melanie as she looked at her menu. Jay came back and they had a wonderful lunch.

The wax museum was a great choice. The three of them had a lovely time and they chose to ride the gondolas at the Venetian Hotel. Italian music played on the sound system as they walked and checked out most of the shops. Jay saw an ice cream shop and treated the ladies to ice cream before finding the pool hall. Luckily all three of them play well at pool so you didn't know who would win the game. The ladies took turns as Jay played every game. Time passed and they walked outside on to the bridge. Jay came up behind Samantha and wrapped his arms around her as they watched the sunset.

The ladies took Jay back to The Bellagio and went home. Melanie turned on the hot tub and they went to put their swim suits on and a few minutes later Melanie poured two glasses of Kendall Jackson chardonnay. Samantha was on the phone with Juan Costas while Melanie waited in the hot tub.

"Thank you for pouring the wine."

"No problem Sugar. Was that Jay?"

"No, it was Juan. We are getting together when I get back home," said Samantha as she smiled and stared at the lit candle on the table. Samantha's phone rang.

"It's Margaret. Should I let it go to voice mail?"

"It's up to you Honey."

Samantha let it go to voice mail and two minutes later she received a 911 text. "This can't be good. I need to call her."

"What's going on Margaret?"

"It's Jack. He was killed in a car accident last night!" Margaret's voice trembled and she could hear her sniffling.

"Oh my God! How did this happen? I can't believe it."

"What happened?" whispered Melanie. Samantha ignored Melanie.

"I'll catch a flight home tonight, ok? I don't want you to be alone."

"You don't have to. I don't know all of the details yet."

"You probably will by the time I get there sweetie. I'm still coming."

"Alright."

"See you soon, goodbye."

"Bye."

"What was that all about Honey?" asked Melanie.

"Jack was killed in a car accident last night."

Melanie looked at Samantha in devastation and tears in her eyes.

CHAPTER 3

Samantha landed in Santa Barbara after catching a red-eye flight from Las Vegas. It was 4 am and the airport looked deserted with only a few flight crew catching their shuttles to hotels near the beach. Samantha flagged down a taxi to get her home. The driver pulled up and she got in and it started to rain; tears from heaven, she thought as she told the driver where to go. Samantha noticed a rosary hanging from the rear-view mirror. She texted Margaret to tell her she was on the way home and also texted Jay to tell him she was no longer in Vegas and left on emergency. Melanie will be out in two days to be with everyone. Juan already heard the news and was on his way to Santa Barbara.

Margaret noticed the cab pull up and helped Samantha with her luggage. They decided to sleep at Samantha's house. Neither one of them wanted to be alone and they stayed up talking until the sun rose.

Jack lost contact with his family several years ago after he dropped out of law school. He came to Santa Barbara to start a new life and this is where his life ended. He died a happy man. In his eyes he was successful. He taught surfing, he was a landscaper, a bartender, and knew his way around the ladies.

Samantha made coffee while Margaret answered phone calls and friends were coming to the area to help make funeral arrangements. Margaret received a call from the towing yard to retrieve Jack's belongings from the wrecked vehicle. The police report indicated he went over the cliff after losing control of the car in the rain. They suspected an animal darted out in front of him according to the skid marks. No other vehicles were involved and the braked were in good condition.

The ladies arrived at the tow yard and it looked like an eerie perdition of crushed metal and shattered glass. They did not want to be there. There were only three items to be claimed. A cell phone, wallet, and a locked brief case.

"Let's take this crap and get out of here. I'm starving," said Margaret in her smoker's voice. She smoked even more when she was upset or emotional. It was only one pm and her first pack was almost gone.

"How can you think of food right now? Our friend just died."

"He wouldn't want us to go hungry. We'll go to *El Torito.* My treat."

"If we must. I'll be drinking. One of us has to stay sober," said Samantha.

The ladies ate and spent most of their time on their phones receiving calls and texting. After lunch the ladies dropped Jack's cell phone off at the police station so they can contact anyone that hasn't been notified on Jack's contact list. To their surprise, an officer found Jack's next-of-kin in Dallas, TX. Her name is Maria and she is Jack's estranged sister. They haven't seen each other in five years and no one has heard of her. Jack never mentioned siblings and if he did it was in passing and no one paid attention. Maria was on the next plane to Santa Barbara and the officer agreed to pick her up. Samantha kept Jack's wallet but decided to turn the brief case over to the police. It was locked and the ladies knew what ever was in there had to be turned in.

Samantha and Margaret went home to Samantha's house to take naps. Samantha went to her room and took a Tylenol PM and laid on her bed and stared at the ceiling. Tears started to roll out of her eyes and to the side of her face. She wanted someone to hold and give her affection. Samantha felt empty and lonely and couldn't wait to see Jay or Juan; who ever got there first. Margaret lied on the sofa with her IPOD and her eyes closed. She was taking this well and seemed to be a lot stronger than Samantha. The pill Samantha took didn't do much good. She only slept twenty minutes. Samantha received a call from Juan and he was thirty minutes away and wanted to meet her at Paradise Café. She nudged Margaret and told her she was leaving soon to meet Juan.

"You can stay here and sleep if you'd like."

"No, but thanks. I'm going to take a walk on the beach to clear my head. If I find any sand dollars, I'll bring them to you."

"Thank you. That's so sweet," replied Samantha.

Samantha arrived at Paradise Café in casual clothing and saw Juan sitting at the bar. There was a female server taking Jack's place as bartender along with an 8" X 10" framed photo of Jack with tea-lite candles and carnations in front of it. It felt so strange not to see Jack behind the bar. Juan stood up and kissed Samantha on the cheek. "Hi sweetheart. You probably didn't get much sleep."

"Not really. Look at the bags under my eyes. At least I don't have to go back to work until all of this is over."

"You still look lovely. Do you know any more details? When is the wake?" asked Juan.

"All I know is Jack's sister should be arriving any minute and the officer will pick her up to take her to the hotel. She is supposed to make all of the arrangements. Margaret and I went to the tow yard and gathered Jack's belongings and I have his wallet. I will give it to her when I meet her. I'm waiting for that call."

"I had no idea Jack had a sister. He never spoke of her."

"I know. I don't think they were very close. She lives in Dallas, TX. Her name is Maria. I don't know anything about her."

"What's Margaret up to?"

"She's walking on the beach. She can't sleep and of course she smoked a lot this morning."

Samantha received a text from Jay and he will do his best to get to Santa Barbara before the funeral. Jack loved the mission and she hopes the funeral and burial will be there. Thirty minutes later Samantha's phone rang. It was the police officer and Maria was being dropped off at Paradise Café. Samantha agreed to take her back to the hotel.

Samantha, Juan, and Maria talked for two hours and they got to know each other. Maria spoke to Jack on the phone a month ago and they agreed to rekindle their toxic relationship and make it loving and substantial. Samantha drove Maria to The Ritz Carlton and made sure she was checked in for the next two weeks and Juan was going to stay at the hotel also.

"How was your meeting with Maria? Is she a decent person?" asked Margaret.

"She seems decent and she's a recovering alcoholic. That's probably why Jack never spoke of her. Maybe he was embarrassed and they also had a falling-out a few years ago. She seems oblivious of Jack's death. She is probably in denial or shock because they spoke not too long ago. Maria and I are meeting for breakfast tomorrow. She wants me to speak at the eulogy," said Samantha.

Margaret handed Samantha a sand dollar that she found on the beach during her walk. It resembled the same one Jack kept behind the bar for good luck. She took this as a sign that Jack's spirit was there. They sat around, had wine, and toasted to Jack. Samantha's phone rang and it was Jay. She excused herself and took the call in the other room. Jay mentioned he was flying into town tomorrow to spend time with Samantha and she invited him to stay in her home. She thought it would be good to break the ice and he could stay in the guest room. Melanie was calling so Samantha excused herself and took the call. Melanie was on her way but would have to stay at The Ritz since Jay was taking the guest room. Juan was also staying at the hotel.

The next morning Samantha met Maria at the hotel restaurant to discuss the details of the funeral. Maria was amazed at the ocean and how the surfers rode the waves without falling. The server poured more coffee for her as she let the wind brush her hair. She can sit there for hours and take it all in.

"Hello Maria. How are you?" asked Samantha as she approached the table.

"It's good to see you again. I'm doing well. Thanks. I slept soundly. The beds are so comfortable here."

"Glad to hear it. Are you hungry?"

"Of course," replied Maria.

"We should order then."

"Once my brother is buried we can all rest and I can start my novation."

"You sound disturbed. Did you find out anything?"

"Oh, I found out plenty. The autopsy report was clean. There was nothing in his system so he wasn't intoxicated. He died instantly of a head injury. No one ran him off the road and it wasn't a hit-and-run. So, it probably was an animal he was trying to avoid. It's a good thing he is dead otherwise I would kick him in the head myself!"

"Why? What happened?" Samantha was stunned at her anger.

"The briefcase you found was filled with cocaine. Jack was a fucking drug dealer!" Tears rolled down her cheeks. "After all he and I have been through; after all of the lectures about my drinking…"

"Oh, Maria. I am so sorry. I never knew this. He was such a good friend to all of us. Are you sure it wasn't planted in his car or a setup?"

"He was a courier. He got paid to deliver," said Maria as she wiped her tears and ordered the Eggs Benedict.

"Then he wasn't using. That makes things a little better."

"Not really. He'd still go to jail. I can't believe he did this."

"I hope the coffee is strong enough for you." Maria grinned as Samantha flagged down the server. "After we eat, we are going to the pool to swim."

"I didn't bring a swim suit."

"I will go to the gift shop and buy you one."

Samantha's phone rang and it was Juan wanting to meet with her in the afternoon and she agreed.

"Would it be alright if Juan meets us at the pool later?"

"Of course, it's alright. Is he your boyfriend?"

Samantha giggled. "Not really. He's a musician. My love interest is Jay who lives in NY. I met him on one of my flights."

The ladies finished their breakfast and Samantha paid the bill. They walked slowly to the gift shop and discussed the funeral.

"Have you thought about what kind of service you want to have?"

"I can't believe my brother was a drug dealer. I'm sorry, what was the question?" Maria looked troubled.

"The service—have you thought about that?"

"Yes, I have. I need to call the mission. He loved that place."

"Let's do that. I'll let you use my phone."

Maria and Samantha sat on a bench outside of the gift shop to make phone calls. They ended up being successful and made an appointment at the mission for tomorrow. Maria stared into the store window and noticed the profligacy that she couldn't afford but she wasn't paying for it so she felt more at ease.

"Did you need anything besides a swimsuit? I can use my airline discount."

"No, I don't think so but thanks for asking."

Maria saw a blue floral one-piece and a red solid one-piece that she liked and headed towards the fitting room. Maria spoke through the door while Samantha returned a text from Juan. He was already at the pool bar ordering a beer.

"I'm trying on the red one first. Ok?"

"Alright. I want to see it."

Maria came out and looked in the mirror. It showed off a dark, slender 5'5" body.

"I don't know about this one. It makes me look like a lifeguard," said Maria as she turned to look at her backside.

"Red is not your color. You should try on the other one."

"I agree."

"You and Jack have similar features but you have dark skin and dark eyes."

"Our mother was Hispanic. She died when we were young so we never learned the language fluently. Jack spoke about 75% of it but couldn't write it and I understand most of it. Oh, I like this blue one much better."

Maria came out and it was a hit. Samantha smiled.

"I love it. You can put your skirt right on top of it. It'll look nice."

Maria put on her white flowing skirt and they were on their way.

The ladies made it outside and Juan waved from the bar with beer in hand.

"Hello ladies. How was breakfast?"

"Tasty," said Samantha.

"Tasteless," said Maria at the same time. "There might be something wrong with my taste buds. Everything seems bland for some reason."

"That is normal. You are going through a lot right now," said Samantha.

"I'll take a diet cola and head over to the hot tub for some alone time. I'm starting to get emotional again," said Maria.

"No problem honey. We understand. We'll be over in a little while."

Maria took her diet soda in a plastic cup, moved her sunglasses from the top of her head to her face and walked slowly with the wind in her face and skirt flowing in the breeze. She looked angelic.

"Do you think she's going to be alright?" asked Juan as he handed Samantha a sparkling water.

"I think so. It's starting to hit her that Jack is gone. This is normal. I think my friend Melanie is going to call any minute. She took a red-eye last night."

Little did they know Melanie spotted them and walked toward the bar with her big hair, big pink hat, big sunglasses, big breasts, and larger-than-life personality.

"Look what the cat dragged in! Here I am, Sugar!"

"Oh, my God! Look at you! I was just talking about you."

"Of course, you were. When people stop talking about me, that's when I'll worry." Juan laughed and Melanie extended her hand. "Hi. I'm Melanie, retired dancer and friend of Sam's."

"Hello. The pleasure is all mine. I'm Juan."

"Oh. I like the sound of that. I think I might have had too much coffee."

"There's a shocker," replied Samantha.

"So, where is this Maria that you speak of? Does she need a Xanax?"

"No! She needs a little space right now. That's her over by the hot tub."

"She looks sweet."

"She is and we are becoming fast friends. Apparently, Jack was no angel."

"Of course not. He was a *bad boy.*"

"you're telling me," Replied Samantha.

"Why? What are you telling me? Did he have someone's wife in the car when he crashed?"

"No. We'll talk about it later."

"Ok, honey."

Most of Jack's friends lived in Santa Barbara and a select few came in from out of town and stayed at The Ritz Carlton. This was like a family reunion for Melanie. She hadn't seen these people in a couple of years and tried to keep her composure due to the circumstances. Maria was spending a lot of time with Juan and asked him to sing and play his clarinet at the funeral. He felt honored. Juan had never played at a funeral and knew exactly which piece to play to please Jack.

It was late afternoon and everyone started to go their separate ways. Samantha headed to the airport to pick up Jay. She received a text from Juan as soon as she parked the car at the airport.

'Billy heard the news about Jack and cancelled his gig in Toronto to be at the funeral.'

Samantha became flush and took a sip of her bottled water and walked quickly towards baggage claim. This was all she needed; a third man to flirt with at the funeral. Luckily Billie has a girlfriend and she can shake him off if he gets too close. It's Juan and Jay that she was worried about. Maria was growing fond of Juan and maybe she'll keep him occupied so she can have some alone time with Jay. Samantha noticed Jay getting his luggage and tapped him on the shoulder. Jay turned around and his chocolate brown eyes met hers.

"Hey, beautiful! Long-time-no-see."

They hugged. Jay had business clothes on with a white button-down dress shirt that was unbuttoned at the top just enough to show some chest hair and his fancy gold chain.

Jay and Samantha drove to the nearest café for a late-night snack and talked for two hours.

"I need to get up early. I promised Maria I'd go with her to the Mission to make funeral arrangements. You should sleep in or enjoy the beach."

"I'm looking forward to seeing your home and how you live."

"I have a next-door neighbor, Margaret, who comes over all of the time. She is retired so she sits on the balcony and smokes and drinks coffee or booze. She is a widow. We've known each other for years," explained Samantha.

"She will keep me entertained while you are away," Jay smiled.

They made it to Samantha's beach house before 10pm and Jay settled into the guest room. He was amazed and impressed at the décor. There were many black and white photos of Samantha and her parents on the wall, an old surf board that Samantha and her father used to share in the corner of the room, and plenty of shells and sand dollars on the window sill. It took him back to the 1980's and how he would spend his Summers in Florida. The bathroom was decorated the same way with sea horse wall paper and matching shower curtain. Jay noticed a clean sand dollar in the corner leaning up against the mirror. He picked it up and turned it over. It read: *5-1-10* in black permanent marker. This was the day they had met at the airport in Florida almost eight weeks ago. He couldn't believe Samantha had kept the sand dollar he had slipped in her bag. It was obvious it meant something to her since it had that special date. Jay smiled and got ready for a good night's sleep.

The small window near the ceiling was just above ground level and brought in enough sunlight so the guest room wouldn't look like a dungeon. It was slightly open so Jay could hear the crashing waves and seagulls. He looked at his cell phone to see the time and it was 9am. Jay couldn't believe he had slept ten glorious hours. He used the restroom, put on his robe, and headed upstairs to the kitchen. The coffee pot had hot coffee with a not next to it written on yellow steno paper:

Darling,
I've gone to the mission with Maria and Melanie. There are bagels
and cream cheese in the refrigerator. Help yourself to what ever
you like. I'll text you soon.
Love, Sam

Jay smiled and smelled a mild scent of menthol as he looked out the window and saw Margaret on her balcony. He fixed his coffee and went outside to meet her. Margaret turned and smiled as she put her cigarette in her ash tray.

"My, aren't you a sight for sore eyes," she said in a raspy voice.

"Hello, I'm Jay."

"I know who you are." She reached out her hand to meet his.

"This is the most beautiful morning I've ever seen. No wonder Sam loves this place. I would never leave," said Jay.

"I don't think she will leave. She's been coming here since she was a little girl. Is this your first visit to Santa Barbara?"

"Yes it is. Do you realize your balconies are only a few inches apart?"

"Five and a half to be exact." There was a small walk-way leading to Margaret's balcony with a gate. "You must have a nice place in New York."

"I live in a penthouse in Manhattan."

"Of course, you do," Margaret giggled as she picked up her cigarette. They spent the rest of the morning chatting.

Maria, Samantha, and Melanie entered the vestibule at the mission and took the elevator to the basement where they met the priest and funeral director. Maria was asked to sign in and go over the arrangements with Fr. Nick. Maria seemed calm as she was picking out flowers and a hearse. Samantha held Maria's hand as she spoke about Jack and what his tastes were. They were offered coffee and sparkling water before heading to the showroom of caskets. Samantha and Melanie locked arms and walked slowly behind Maria and Fr. Nick. Samantha whispered to Melanie, "She seems calm. What did you give her?"

"I gave her a Valium."

"What?! Are you crazy? You just met the woman and you're already giving her drugs?"

Melanie smiled, "She needed it. That's the only way she'll get through this. Drugs, booze, and sex."

"She's a recovering alcoholic."

"Ok, forget the booze. We'll just find her a hot guy."

They entered the room full of caskets with mannequins inside of them. Solemn piano music played on the speakers and the sunlight broke through the stained-glass window. Maria stood in silence. Samantha stroked her hair. "Are you ok honey?" asked Samantha.

"Yes—yes, of course. Let's get this over with."

"This brings back memories. I knew I should have brought my flask," said Melanie as a small tear rolled down her left cheek.

CHAPTER 4

It was a beautiful Sunday morning in Santa Barbara and not a cloud in the sky. The Ritz Carlton lay on a cliff looking over the Pacific Ocean with the Sea Breeze Café attached to the hotel with endless windows looking over the water. A small island with a lighthouse was two miles in the distance. Samantha, Melanie, Maria, Margaret, Jay, and Juan all sat at a nice table for champagne brunch before the funeral. Nice words about Jack were exchanged throughout the meal and everyone wore black except Jay. He had a navy blue suit on with a silver dress shirt. Jay almost didn't attend the service because he never met Jack. He was here to support Samantha and volunteered to be a poll bearer. Jay obviously won her heart by doing this. Samantha sat between Jay and Juan and could feel the tension between them. Margaret looked at Samantha with a silly smirk and excused herself from the table to have a cigarette and Jay tried to make small talk with Juan.

"So, Juan, I hear your music in some of the jazz clubs and also on the radio in New York City. You have many fans. Do you have any gigs in the near future?" asked Jay as he put his hand on Samantha's lap.

"As a matter of fact, I just cancelled a show to be here and I'm off to Key Largo, FL in a couple of days."

Juan winked at Maria across the table and Melanie was enjoying all of the drama and kept smiling as she grabbed a bottle of champagne from the waiter's cart and poured for everyone except Maria. Some of them topped it off with OJ to make Mimosas and everyone was silent for a moment. Maria was anxious to speak.

"So, does everyone here know that Jack was in a little trouble?" asked Maria. Everyone started speaking at once. They knew what she was referring to. Margaret returned from smoking to see everyone bickering and Maria was trying to listen to each opinion but couldn't understand anyone.

"What the fuck?! What's going on? I leave for a few minutes and everyone has to argue. We should speak one at a time so everything is out in the open. Melanie, you start."

Melanie quickly popped a Xanax in her mouth and took a sip of Mimosa.

"This kind of thing happens all the time in Vegas. I didn't know Jack as well as you guys knew him so I don't have an opinion. Who's next?" Melanie looked at Juan before he spoke.

"I suspected something was going on and I asked him about it but he kept his mouth shut so I just went about my business. I see drugs all the time in my line of work and never saw him using. Sam, what do you think?"

"The autopsy came out clean so he wasn't using; just dealing. I didn't suspect a thing. It would have put a huge strain on our friendship if I would have known," said Samantha.

"I never met him so I'm not going to say anything. I don't judge," said Jay.

"I don't know what to say, really. He never got caught as far as we know. Everyone makes mistakes and we should be at peace with it. Everything happens for a reason," said Margaret as she flagged down the waiter to get the bill.

"Thank you everyone for being such a big part in Jack's life. He was so lucky to have friends like you. Jack had sent me a large check three weeks ago to help me with my business. I sent him a 'thank you' note and promised to visit soon. I didn't know it would be under these circumstances. Jack will be paying for this breakfast and we should be going soon. The limo is waiting outside," Maria said as she put her credit card in the waiter's book and handed it to him.

The six of them got into the limo and headed for the mission. Samantha opened her purse and pulled out her flash cards to rehearse the eulogy while Maria pulled out her rosary, closed her eyes, and prayed silently. Melanie and Margaret held hands and Jay and Juan played a game on their smart phones.

When the limo arrived at the Santa Barbara Mission Juan let the ladies get out first then he quickly got out and proceeded to the oak tree where Billy was standing so they can practice singing 'Ave Maria'. The ladies went over to the hearse and spoke with friends. Everyone was dressed nice in dark clothes and some ladies donned big beautiful hats.

Friends from Paradise Café piled into the church and Maria was the only relative of Jack's that was there. The family lost touch with relatives years ago and Maria knew these people were her family now. She was touched by the beautiful flowers and the love from the people that were there. She hadn't met any of these people until a few days ago. The poll bearers lined up behind the hearse to put the oak casket on the cart so they can wheel it to the foyer. Everything seemed to move in slow motion as in a scene of a movie. Maria thought about dry ice to make fog that way this would be a dream instead of reality. Maria and Samantha locked arms and followed behind the casket while everyone in the church stood up and Billy played the piano and sang a religious song in Latin. It was the most beautiful church Maria had ever seen with stained glass windows, marble floors, flowers, and the smell of incense. The walk to the front of the church felt like the longest walk of her life and Fr. Nick asked everyone to be seated. He spoke nice words of life and how we must celebrate every day because it is such a gift and death is a new beginning. He blessed the casket and sprinkled holy water while the altar boys swung their chains of incense and it was time for Samantha to speak the eulogy. She walked slowly past the casket, kissed her hand and then touched the casket with the same hand and managed to make it to the podium without tripping in her stiletto heels.

"Good afternoon, everyone and thank you for coming. My name is Samantha. Most of you know me as Sam. I knew Jack for over four years and he was a kind and gentle soul; always happy and smiling; a real people pleaser. He was good at everything he did."

Some ladies giggled in the background.

"Yes, even that too; so, I've heard. Jack was always there when you needed him. He was a good listener, a good bartender, a great surfer, a terrific landscaper, and most of all, a wonderful friend. Jack had many friends and no enemies. He was taken from us a bit too soon but I believe he is watching over all of us and he brought his beautiful sister to us and she will remain a great friend. I'm deeply touched by her perseverance and strength during this time. I will continue to see Jack in many ways. When I see a man surfing, I will think of Jack. When I see a beautiful front yard full of flowers, I will think of Jack. When some-one pours me a great martini, I will think of him also. God, I know you have welcomed him into heaven with open arms despite his faults and I hope there's plenty of sand and sea for him to surf in. And the next time I find a sand dollar on the beach I will know it is Jack saying 'hello'. We miss you already and we love you very much. Take care and we'll see you soon enough." A tear rolled down Samantha's cheek as she stepped away from the podium and she could hear the sniffles coming from friends. Billy started to play the piano and Juan sang 'Ave Maria' along with Billy. Maria closed her eyes and remembered how Jack would sing this to her when she was young to help her sleep. She held her rosary tight as everyone stood up to exit the church. Maria followed the pall-bearers carrying the casket back to the hearse. This was the perfect time for Margaret to sneak a cigarette and for Melanie to pop another pill before going to the burial ground up the road.

Maria and Samantha held hands again in the limo and Maria rolled down the window to smell the roses in the church garden as the limo pulled away.

"I'm glad we chose the Mission cemetery so there is no procession. I don't like to draw attention," said Maria.

"When I die, I'm having an extravagant funeral. The procession will be long and drawn out. We'll have a large party at a fancy hotel with an ice sculpture and champagne. We'll serve shrimp and lobster---"said Melanie with a smile to break the somber moment. Everyone laughed; including the driver.

"I hope you put this in your will so I can do this for you," replied Samantha.

"Oh, it's there honey. I'll give you a copy along with a trust to pay for it all."

"You guys make me laugh. I'm so glad I met you. I don't want to sound capricious but I think I'll be ready to pick out a plaque for Jack this week. I want to do this before I go back to Dallas. I don't want this decision hanging over my head."

Juan stared at Maria. His attraction to her became stronger. He didn't know if it was because everyone was vulnerable this week or if he really enjoyed getting to know her. Words played in his head and he thought about writing a song when he got back to the hotel.

The burial was short and sweet and there was one chair for Maria to sit in and everyone else gathered around. There were approximately fifty people and everything seemed to be moving in slow motion. The clouds rolled in and the sound of thunder came from the distance as the casket was being lowered into the ground. Maria dropped a handful of daisies on top of the oak casket as the Lord's Prayer came to a close. She slowly walked to the limo with Samantha without looking back and everyone followed to their own cars and on to the reception at Paradise Café.

The night club was dimly lit with candles at every table and a giant ice sculpture of a sand dollar on the buffet table. Jack's photo was framed at the end of the bar along with two martini glasses filled with small seashells. His surfboard was donated to the club and it leaned up against the wall by the stage. Jack thought about owning this club one day if it was ever put up for sale. Paradise Café was owned by a college professor, Dr. Gwen King. She hardly ever visited the place because she was busy with her own psychology practice and teaching at the university. She didn't attend the funeral but she was at the reception and no one recognized her except for Juan.

"Good afternoon, Dr. King. I'm delighted to be greeted by your presence," Juan said as he shook her hand.

"The pleasure is all mine. I'm sorry to hear about Jack. He was a good man and never spoke badly of anyone. He will be missed."

"This is quite a spread. Thank you for doing this. It means a lot to everyone. This is Maria, Jack's sister." Dr. King and Maria shook hands.

"I've heard nothing but good things about you. Your brother was a patient of mine, you know. I don't think anyone knew he was in therapy."

"I had no idea."

"Well then, we have a lot to talk about." The three of them proceeded to the bar.

CHAPTER 5

Maria woke up to the sound of crashing waves and the warmth of Juan by her side. Two weeks have gone by and it was time to get back to Dallas for her new project. Everyone had gone home and back to their lives; even Samantha had gone back to work a couple of days ago flying around the country. Maria heard Fleetwood Mac playing on the pool-side speakers outside the balcony and went outside to enjoy her coffee. Juan had seen Maria on the balcony with her white silk robe flowing in the wind and came up behind her to embrace the vision and wrap his arms around her.

"I'm going to miss this place," said Maria.

"Then don't go. Stay here. You have everything you need right here."

"You don't even live here. You live in L.A."

"I'm going to buy a house here. We can be roommates," Juan said with a smile.

"You're crazy. We can't be roommates. It would ruin our friendship and I'm opening my jewelry store soon. I'm going home to sign the lease. My flight is in four hours."

"Are you feeling alright about life and what it has brought you? You've made some nice friends here."

"I know. It's incredible. I'm just thinking about Jack and his short comings. I think he meant well; he just got involved with the wrong people and he was in over his head." Maria went in the bathroom to get ready while Juan helped her pack. Maria received a text from Samantha while she was in the shower.

Juan drove Maria to the airport and she was very quiet in the car.

"Sam sent me a text. She'll be in Dallas tomorrow. We're going to try to do lunch."

"That sounds good. I should make plans to come visit you sometime," said Juan.

Juan dropped Maria off at the curb and paid the Sky Cap to take her luggage. They kissed and he got back in the car and headed South back to Los Angeles.

CHAPTER 6

Maria sat in a booth reading a novel at a local Mexican restaurant in Dallas while she waited for Samantha. The bartender made eye contact with Maria and smiled. He reminded her of Jack and it brought tears to her eyes. She looked down and kept on reading. Maria was tempted to start eating the chips and salsa. Samantha knew exactly where to find her so she wasn't worried about texting her. A few minutes later Samantha arrived and the owner greeted her at the door.

"Hola señora. Table for one?"

"No. Actually, I'm meeting my friend here."

"Oh, sí. Right this way." The owner knew exactly who she was meeting. "I'm going to bring you complimentary guacamole for you two lovely ladies."

"Muchas gracias," replied Maria.

"Wow, what a cute place. I love this," Samantha said as she hugged Maria.

"It's my favorite restaurant in town. You look great for being a career woman."

"Thanks, you too. I had time to freshen up. They gave me a room at the Hyatt. I don't fly out until tomorrow afternoon."

"I'm going to the spa in the morning. Would you like to come with me? I can get you an appointment for a massage," said Maria as the owner brought the guacamole.

"That would be amazing. I haven't had one in so long. So how are you holding up? You look terrific by the way. Juan sent me a text and says he misses you. The two of you really hit it off and I thought he and I would date and then I met Jay and everything changed."

"I do miss him too. He asked me to move to California to be with him." Samantha looked surprised and happy.

"You should do it! Did you sign the lease for the jewelry store yet?"

"No. I've been stalling. Don't you think it's risky for me to move? My roots are here," said Maria.

"What roots? No offense but your immediate family is gone and you don't have a boyfriend here in Texas and life is all about taking risks. Juan is a great guy; not to mention smart and good-looking."

"I know. The women love him too. Musicians have a reputation."

"All men do; not just the musicians," Samantha laughed.

"I'll wait a few days and see how I feel before signing the lease. Juan thinks we can live in Santa Barbara together. We'll see if he's serious. It's all fast for me."

"You don't have to marry him. Men are like cars. You have to take them for a test drive." Samantha changed the subject as she browsed the menu. "The quesadilla looks good. I haven't had one of those in a while.

I try making them at home by using cheese slices and corn tortillas and popping them in the microwave," Samantha said with a smile.

"Please tell me you don't do that."

"I call it 'The Flight Attendant Special'."

"Do you think I will be able to open a store in Santa Barbara? Wouldn't the rent be super high?"

"It'll be a little high but I have connections on locations and also you will sell more to make up for the cost. Tell me about some of the items you are selling."

A gambit by Samantha put the conversation at ease as they ordered their lunch. They both enjoyed the Mariachi music and both of their cell phones vibrated at the same time. It was the men in their lives so they let it go to voice mail. There is nothing like two women bonding over lunch.

"A lot of my jewelry is gems, silver, gold, and a few diamonds. The most expensive piece is an Emerald and Diamond ring for $8,000. The jewelry is in a safe deposit box at the bank. I would have to ship it to California if I decide to move there and the insurance would be crazy."

"It sounds like you need to do some planning. Is Juan pressuring you for a time frame?"

"Not exactly. He knows it's a big step."

The ladies ate their lunch and left the waiter a nice tip. Maria wanted to drive Samantha to her hotel three miles down the road. She put the top down on the convertible and they both enjoyed the wind in their hair. Maria couldn't stop thinking about California and how great it would be to live there. She has bonded tightly with Juan and Samantha; she'd be a fool not to go. Maria dropped Samantha off and agreed to see her at the spa in the morning. Samantha went up to her room and unlocked the door and slipped her heels off her nicely pedicured feet when she got in the door and proceeded to the phone to order a bottle of Merlot from room service. She turned on the satellite radio to a smooth jazz station and started a bubble bath. The music was almost too sexy to spend the evening alone. She wished Jay was there to take care of her needs even though they have never consummated their relationship. Samantha was quite ready now and wanted to tell Jay the next time she saw him. There was a knock at the door and she signed for the wine. The gentleman locked eyes with Samantha.

"I'm only going to need one glass," Samantha said seductively as half her left breast showed through the robe.

"That's too bad," said the room server. He couldn't take his Latino eyes off of her. "Call me if you need anything else."

"Of course I will." Samantha closed the door slowly and felt the heat on the back of the door with her palm. She proceeded to the bathroom with the wine and felt the cool marble floor beneath her feet. Samantha put her hair up in a clip and disrobed. She stared at her naked body in the mirror for a moment before lighting the candles. She took a sip of wine and turned off the lights and imagined Jay's arms around her waist. She slowly got into the tub with her glass of wine and her cell phone and called Jay.

"Hello stranger. I'm so glad you picked up. Guess what I'm doing?"

"So glad you called. You must be having a nice time in Dallas. When are you going home?"

"I leave tomorrow afternoon. Maria and I are going to the spa in the morning. I'm in the bathtub with a glass of wine and I'm a little tipsy."

"I presume you are alone."

Samantha giggled. "Of course. My hand is where your hand should be. I'm ready to take this relationship to the next level. This *is* a relationship we are having, right?" Samantha spoke seductively.

"Yes. Are you teasing me or is this phone sex? You're going to make me visit you soon aren't you?"

"I know a cute little beach house in Santa Barbara where you and I can stay for as long as we like."

"Are you working this weekend?"

"No. Are you?"

"I'm always working but I'm the boss remember? I can take off whenever I want."

"Then I will see you tomorrow evening. I'll book your flight."

"Sounds like a plan. I can't wait to see you. I better go. I'm at work and the chef wants to have a word with me, as usual."

"Bye lover."

"Bye honey."

Samantha couldn't take the grin off of her face. This was the happiest she's been in years.

A stream of sun light came through the window between the drapes. Samantha was sound asleep with her sleeping mask on her face when the hotel phone rang. She slowly reached for the phone and put the receiver to her ear. The digital voice spoke.

"Good morning. This is your wake-up call. It is now 8:00 am. Room Service will deliver in 30 minutes. Have a good day. Goodbye."

The voice was monotone and rather boring but she got up anyway and gave Maria a call.

Samantha and Maria sat in the tranquility room and sipped tea after their massages.

"That was truly amazing. Now I can fly home relaxed and wait for Jay to get there."

"You look well rested. To be honest with you, I cried a little during the massage. I was thinking about Jack."

"You are still grieving. It takes time. Have you talked to Juan?"

"I have. I think I have made my decision to move."

"That's amazing! Everyone will be so happy. Is Juan going to help you?"

"Yes. There is nothing keeping me here in Dallas and I know I will enjoy Santa Barbara. I know Jack would want me to move if he was still here."

"Are you still upset about his offense? It was a mistake that cost him his life but you will feel better once you move past it." Samantha placed her hand on Maria's knee and placed a piece of chocolate on her saucer. Maria smiled.

"I think I can forgive him now and accept everything."

"That's a healthy approach. You can't change the past. Everything is falling into place and everything happens for a reason. We all miss Jack but look at the friendships and relationships you have now. You wouldn't have these if Jack didn't pass away."

"I feel like I still need counseling once I move. This is such a huge step and my life has changed so much in the past few weeks."

"I can help you with that. Dr. King is a great therapist and Jack was also a patient of hers," said Samantha.

"Wouldn't that be creepy?"

"Not at all. She would understand you better since she knew Jack. She doesn't talk bosh either. Dr. King is pleasant and professional," said Samantha as she finished her tea and excused herself to the showers.

CHAPTER 7

The sun was setting as the aircraft came in for a landing. Samantha spoke to her colleagues and was the last to exit the plane. A few of them made plans to meet at Paradise Café for drinks and invited Samantha to come along. She agreed but would arrive later on after Jay's arrival. Samantha put on her CHANEL sunglasses and proceeded to her car. The clouds were a dusty pink and the wind was just right as it whistled through the palm trees. She felt like the luckiest woman alive to be living in such a beautiful town. Samantha rolled down all of the windows and breathed in the salty air while listening to smooth jazz. She stopped at a red light and a young man waved at her from his car. She had never seen him before and realized it was just innocent flirting; a nice gesture to be appreciated. Samantha looked to her left and saw college students playing volley ball and drove another half mile to see an artist selling his paintings on the sidewalk. State Street had everything to offer. From bars to psychic readers, old book stores, and small spas. There was no time to be bored and Santa Barbara was always reinventing itself. Margaret noticed Samantha pulling in to her driveway and waved at her while exhaling a puff of smoke from her Salem cigarette. Samantha hurried inside to meet her on the balcony.

"I've missed you these past few days. Would you like a glass of wine?" asked Margaret in a hoarse voice.

"You read my mind. I have good news."

"Good for me? Or good for you?"

"It depends on how you look at it. First of all, Jay is coming here tonight and he is staying the weekend. Second, Maria is leaving her life in Dallas and moving here to Santa Barbara and third, my colleagues are having drinks at Paradise Café tonight and we are invited. Are you up to it?"

Margaret had never seen Samantha so happy. "You look like you are ready to burst with happiness. Of course, I'll go. Are we waiting for Jay?"

"Yes. He'll be here in an hour."

"I bet Juan has something to do with Maria moving here."

"Yes, they're an item now," said Samantha as she sipped her Chardonnay.

"He better not fuck this one up. Maria's a nice lady."

"He's grown since his divorce two years ago. He won't let his job control his life anymore."

"What about the groupies? They will throw themselves at him again, you know?"

"That's inevitable. He's a musician and I'm sure Maria will get used to it. I'm going to freshen up. I'll see you in an hour," said Samantha.

Samantha took her glass of wine and went inside. Her phone rang and it was Melanie. She chatted with her for almost four minutes while choosing an outfit. Samantha turned on New Age music and found dark eye shadow to put on to match her sequence top. Forty five minutes went by and her wine glass was empty. She put the final touches of lip gloss on her pouty lips and headed to the balcony. Samantha looked at Margaret in her denim outfit and she never looked better.

"Wow, you clean up real nice."

"Of course. I want to look nice for the fly girls. It's been a while since I've seen them."

"They haven't changed. Maybe one of them will bring a pilot," smiled Samantha.

"That wouldn't surprise me."

Samantha received a text from Jay. He was on his way in a limo.

"We don't have to drive tonight. Jay got a limo. He'll probably say he couldn't find a taxi. If I had his money, I wouldn't bother with a taxi either."

"I better put out my cigarette before he gets here. I shouldn't smoke in front of him. He's too classy," said Margaret.

Jay arrived and freshened up in the bathroom. Samantha knocked on the door with a glass of Merlot in her hand that was only a third full. He chugged it quickly and they were on their way. Samantha received a text from Juan.

Hey Sam, I'm coming to town next weekend to look at two houses. See you then :)

Samantha replied: *Fantastic!*

They arrived at Paradise Café in fashion. The flight attendants had a table already in the corner. There were two female flight attendants, one male flight attendant, and one male pilot who was probably married but no one really knew the real story behind his tan skin and green eyes. He made the women melt. There was a DJ instead of a band and people were dancing and having a great time. Samantha was pretty sure Juan was going to play here next weekend. She popped a pretzel into her mouth and kissed Jay and checked her phone for another text. This time it was from Melanie:

Juan is playing at Paradise Café next weekend. I'll be there. I'm staying at The Ritz as usual.

Samantha realized that next weekend was Labor Day weekend and the town will be hopping. She returned the text:

I'm so glad! I'll see you then.

Samantha looked at the bar and saw Jack's picture and then looked at his surf board behind the stage and for the first time she wasn't sad about Jack. He would have wanted everyone to continue with their lives and have a great time.

A cool breeze came through the curtains of Samantha's bedroom window. She can hear the waves crashing in the distance as she lay naked in her satin sheets next to Jay. Samantha realized she still had her jewelry on from last night so she got up and walked to her dresser, which had a large mirror, and removed her bracelet and diamond stud earrings and proceeded to the bathroom to start the shower. She glanced at Jay while he slept and she smiled in the mirror. Samantha had never felt happier in her 37 years. It was still early, 7:55 to be exact, but not too early for Margaret to take a walk on the beach. While Samantha showered, Jay slept and Margaret walked and watched joggers with their dogs. This was an incredible life they all had. Margaret went back to her balcony for a cigarette and watched a beautiful yacht sail by in the distance. Jay woke up and went to the kitchen to make coffee and noticed Margaret on her balcony.

"Hey stranger," said Jay. Margaret put out her cigarette immediately.

"Good morning. What a night we had. I haven't had that much fun in years," said Margaret.

"Seriously? You should get out more. It's good for you."

"I know. I'm such a home-body. Look at this view. Can you blame me?"

"I made coffee. Would you like some?"

"Sounds good. Is Sam still sleeping?"

"No. She's in the shower. This is quite a view. I think it beats staring at the Empire State Building every morning."

"Get out. You have a view of the Empire State Building?"

"I live on the 30th floor of my building. I inherited the penthouse from my father. I couldn't have got the place on my own. He was heavy into real estate. He was popular in the 1970's."

"It sounds amazing. I haven't been to New York City since I was a kid. I was probably 5 or 6 years old."

"You're welcome anytime. Just bring Sam. It's beautiful around the holidays and the people are friendlier."

Samantha peeked out on the balcony with just a towel on her head.

"I just spoke to Maria. She is coming here next weekend. I finally realized it's a holiday weekend and that's why everyone wants to be here. Jay, are you interested in coming? I know it's a long haul for you."

"I'll see how the restaurant is doing and if they can live without me. Do you know if Juan plays golf? That would entice me."

"He sure does," said Samantha.

"Ok. I'll be sure to bring my golf shoes if I can make it."

Monday rolled around and the town was quiet and only the surf made its presence known. Samantha worked short shifts this week and didn't have to stay overnight anywhere but was prepared to. She spent every day with Margaret going to the gym, playing pool, and having tasty lunches. One day, after having lunch at Paradise Café, they took a walk along the beach and found a starfish.

"What do we have here?" asked Margaret as she picked it up. "I've never found one of these before. It will go perfect in my bathroom."

"Every time we find sand dollars I always think Jack is around saying 'hello' to us. It's a spiritual thing. I wonder what the starfish means," said Samantha.

"I don't know but if I ever find another, I will give it to you."

"Thank you! That means a lot."

Friday rolled around and tourists were flying in from all over the country and the airport was packed. Melanie was one of the last passengers to exit the plane and she mumbled to herself, "What the fuck? Why are all of these people here? I'm going to need a drink soon. This is ludicrous."

She walked by a Starbucks and saw a familiar face putting Splenda in her coffee.

"Maria? Oh my God, it *is* you! You look fabulous."

"Hi! I'm so glad you are here. I really missed everyone. Are you staying at The Ritz?"

"You know it. I wouldn't stay anywhere else. And you?"

"The same. Juan got us a nice room. He'll be here later. He wants to look at houses tomorrow."

"It sounds like we have catching up to do. Let's share a cab. My treat."

Maria smiled at the idea and they both went off to baggage claim.

The sun had already dipped into the ocean and dusk was upon the town as Samantha watered her plants on the balcony waiting for a text from Jay. All of the others have contacted her except Jay.

Juan was very relaxed driving his convertible North on Highway 1 with the top down and just a touch of sunscreen on his unshaven face. To his left were surfers packing their boards to leave and to his right were the rolling hills of Ventura County covered with wildflowers. He had another 10 miles before he reached Santa Barbara and the woman that he loved. Juan was looking forward to playing golf this weekend with Jay but wasn't absolutely sure if he was coming on such short notice. Melanie and Maria had already checked in to The Ritz Carlton and were sitting pool-side bonding over drinks. Maria has been sober over three years and enjoyed her Diet Coke and hasn't craved a drink since the night Jack died. Her sponsor kept her straight and she never fell off the wagon.

Jay looked out his Manhattan penthouse window with a scotch on the rocks in his left hand and saw how hard it was raining. He sent a text to Samantha and said his flight was cancelled due to the storm but never actually checked the website to see if it was. He walked over to the fireplace and stared into the flames before pouring himself another drink. He looked out the window once more and saw the reflection of the woman in his bed. She sat up and covered her large breasts with the silk sheet and said, "Come back to bed sweetie. I need you next to me."

CHAPTER 8

Samantha and the gang waited outside Paradise Café for a table to have lunch. Dr. King was behind the bar helping the bartender and noticed Maria through the window and went outside to say hello.

"Hello everyone! I had no idea all of you were coming for lunch. I'll get you a table right away."

The Beatles were playing on the stereo and the mist kept everyone cool outside. It was in the high 80's and there was nothing but joy and laughter in the air. Samantha received a text from Jay and he was at JFK airport catching the next plane to Santa Barbara. The table was ready and they walked past the bar with Jack's picture and they were able to sit near the closed stage by Jack's surfboard. The place looked more tropical. Dr. King had decorated with large pictures of surfers and wooden birds were hanging from the ceiling.

"The band is playing tonight, Juan. Do you want to join them for a short set? They would love to have you," asked Dr. King.

"Thank you doc but I need to run it buy Maria first," said Juan as he looked at Maria.

"Of course, honey. It would make you happy and the band as well."

"We are looking at two houses today after lunch," said Juan to Dr. King.

"Are you finally moving here? That's fantastic! Congratulations. It will inspire you to write more songs."

"Maria is moving here with me."

"I knew you two would hit it off."

All five of them finished their lunch and went to the first open house nestled in the hills overlooking the Mission. The house was modern and had a huge balcony with an 80-foot-long swimming pool.

"Mel, this house is bigger than yours," said Samantha as she went up the winding staircase.

"It's more expensive too. It must have something to do with the location. Did you see the price on the flyer?"

"Its 2.5 million dollars! Can Juan afford this?" whispered Samantha.

"Of course. His last album sold a billion copies or something. He has more money than God. Most people don't recognize him because he's a jazz musician. It's an elite crowd. Wait until Jazz Fest in the Fall. All of his groupies will come out."

"We're with a celebrity. I can't believe it," said Margaret.

"I had no idea he was that famous. We've known him as acquaintance for so long it's like we're family," said Samantha.

"All six of us are family now. Too bad Jay couldn't make it," said Melanie.

"He's on his way. He'll be here tonight."

Off they went to the next house. This one was closer to the beach and more expensive. Margaret was enjoying the snacks they were serving.

"We should go house hunting every weekend. These sandwiches are great."

"How can you eat? We just had lunch an hour ago," said Samantha.

"I'm trying to quit smoking so I'm stuffing my face. Now I'm going to get fat."

"No, you won't darling. Just exercise more. Take advantage of the beach. It's right in your backyard," said Melanie.

Melanie looked at Juan and Maria holding hands on the balcony and talking to the real estate agent. "Who would have thought Jack's death would bring these two love birds together. They make a great couple. How do you feel about these two as a couple Margaret? Are you feeling surfeit from the snacks?"

"How did you know? I think they are great together. Are you going back to Paradise Café tonight? It's Beatles night. Do you think Juan can pull it off? It's not really his style."

"He's a man of many talents. Don't count on Sam. Jay is flying in tonight and they might want to be alone," said Melanie.

They all went back to The Ritz and talked pool-side about the beautiful homes they saw. The second home was massive for just two people and the rumor was the previous owner died by suicide in the garage. The price was four million dollars. A hefty price for a house that may be haunted. Juan and Maria put their feet in the hot tub and sat on the edge. Maria mentioned how she had to find a new sponsor here in town and go to AA meetings. They also discussed the name of her jewelry store. She wanted the store to remind her of Jack in some way since he gave her the money to start her own business. Maria needed to stay a few more days so she can look at vacant shops.

Jay arrived at the Santa Barbara airport before sundown and caught a cab to Samantha's house. He didn't bother to text her and his communication skills were failing. All he could think about is how he lied to her and slept with another woman. The guilt was getting to him. He arrived to Samantha's house to find no one home so he called her.

"Hello? Hi Jay!"

"I'm at your house. Where are you?"

"I'm at The Ritz with everyone else."

"Well, the cab just took off so I'm stuck in your front yard."

Samantha was surprised by his irritated behavior. *"I'll be there in a few minutes. I'm leaving now."*

"Fine. Ok." Jay hung up abruptly and Samantha excused herself to go home.

When Samantha arrived, Jay smiled and hugged her tight. They decided not to go out in the evening. Jay wanted to spend time with Samantha alone and even bought massage oil at the airport so he can treat her to a massage. They ordered Chinese food and watched a movie before the massage.

"Did Juan get in touch with you about playing golf tomorrow?"

"Yes, he did. We are playing at 1:00."

"Did you know he is playing with the band tonight at Paradise Café?"

"No, he didn't mention it."

"He probably didn't want to sound conceited," said Samantha.

Everyone was having a fabulous time at Paradise Café listening to Beatles songs. Juan never lost his touch playing the oldies.

"It's too bad Jay and Sam couldn't make it," said Margaret as the band played 'Day Tripper'.

"Jay probably has jet lag. He was just here last week and he's been working," said Maria in his defense.

Juan began to sing 'Hey Jude' but changed the lyrics to 'Hey Jack' and changed some of the words about Jack being in heaven and the people he is with. Maria cried unexpectedly. Juan thought this up during the day. That's how talented he was. He could write a song in a matter of minutes and turn it into a hit. Now the girls really wished Samantha and Jay were here to witness it. The band ended their set with 'The Long and Winding Road' and 'Something' which Juan dedicated to Maria. She knew then he was a keeper. Margaret and Melanie considered her the luckiest woman in town.

Everyone met at The Ritz for breakfast. They even had the same server they had before on the day of the funeral. It felt like de` ja vu. Maria bragged to Jay and Samantha about how great Juan was last night at the club.

"I'm sorry we missed it. I was just beat. It was a long week for me but I am looking forward to golf this afternoon," said Jay with his unshaven face and dark circles under his eyes. He even looked as though he lost three or four pounds since they last saw him. Jay received a text from the other woman he was with two nights ago. She was an intern chef at his restaurant and hoped it was just a one-night stand. There was no way he could juggle two women and run a restaurant. He didn't return the text until later.

The boys made it to the golf course while the ladies went shopping and spent extra time at Starbucks talking about Maria's future in this new town.

"So, you decided to move here; that's great. Are you going to look at vacant shops for your store? You won't have any trouble. I guarantee it," said Margaret with confidence.

"As soon as Juan goes back to Los Angeles, I will get busy. I will also fly to Dallas and get the rest of my things. I want to name the shop 'Sand Dollar Jewelers'. What do you think of that name?"

The women smiled and looked at each other. "We love it," said Melanie.

Melanie changed the subject to Samantha and Jay. "So, Sam, how is Jay feeling these days? He looks worn out. Maybe he should stay put in New York City for a while so he doesn't get burned out and you can visit him. I'm just throwing that out there honey. You don't want an exhausted man because then he won't be able to get it up. If you know what I'm saying."

"I know what you mean but he seems to be fine in that department."

The ladies finished their coffee and did more walking down State Street. They found a candle shop and went inside. Maria noticed a vacant shop across the street and wrote down the phone number.

"It smells so good in here. I can buy one of each," said Margaret as she noticed Maria jotting down the number.

"What day do you have to leave for Dallas?" asked Melanie.

"I leave Tuesday evening. Juan is leaving Tuesday morning to drive back to Los Angeles. He might keep his town home there so he has a place to stay on the days he is recording."

"Will you look at more homes in the near future?" asked Samantha.

"We will discuss that tonight. What is the plan for this evening anyway?" asked Maria.

The ladies looked at Margaret as though she had the answer.

"I take it you want me to decide. We should take a walk on the beach while the men are cooling down from golf. We'll stop at the store on the way home to pick up chicken and I will barbeque on the deck. Sam, you should text the boys to see if this plan works for them."

"I can do that."

The boys were at the 16th hole and having a great time talking and giving each other advice on strategy. Jay's cell phone was on vibrate and he took it off his holster and turned it off.

"The restaurant must need you right now," said one of the players.

"Actually, it's my intern chef Stacey. She probably has questions about tonight's menu."

The whore finally has a name. She's a large chested woman, 5'10", golden tan, blonde hair, and happens to be from Florida. She's doing her internship at Jay's restaurant hoping to move up the ladder by sleeping with him. Jay only feels a small amount of guilt. He figures if you're not living with a woman it's ok to do as you please. Samantha doesn't know this and wasn't raised that way. They have taken their relationship to a new level and have talked about being exclusive.

The men finished their golf game and Jay won by a hair. They talked and showered in the locker room. While Jay was getting dressed, he called Stacey back.

"I'm in California visiting family. I'll be home Tuesday morning. I miss you too. I'll text you later. Bye for now," said Jay as he hung up the phone and saw Juan come around the corner.

The men arrived at the house and the aroma smelled delicious. Margaret was half-way finished barbequing the chicken while Jay took over. Bob Marley was playing on the stereo and everyone was swaying to the music with their drinks.

"Mel, have you thought about coming back here to live? Don't you miss it?" asked Samantha.

"I've thought about it. Maybe I can live in both places. I don't want to sell my home in Vegas. I have a lot of friends there and there's nothing like Vegas. It has everything."

"Except the beach," Margaret interrupted. "If I fix up my guest room will you consider living with me?"

"That's a fantastic idea," said Jay as he took a swig of his Corona. Juan and Maria were drinking Ginger ale since Maria was an alcoholic. Juan stopped drinking in front of Maria when they became more serious. He only drinks with the guys.

"Do I have time to think about this offer? You're not going to rent the room out to someone else right away?"

"No. The room is cluttered and I need an excuse to clean it up and donate the items."

"I can help you with that, Sugar."

The friends all gathered at Paradise Café for brunch before Maria and Juan looked at another home. This was their last meal together as a group before going their separate ways. Juan had to get back to L.A., Jay had to get back to NY, Melanie had to catch a flight back to Vegas, and Maria was staying one more night to see the vacant shop in the morning.

Dr. King stopped by the table with a pot of coffee half-way through their meal. "It's nice to see you keeping me in business. How is the house hunting?"

They all smiled and said 'hello' and Samantha hugged Dr. King since she was up walking back from the rest room.

"We looked at two homes and we have one more to look at today. Do you know anything about the Cliff Side Manor? We looked at that one but it was too large and too expensive," said Juan.

"Yes. I'll call it the John Doe estate since I can't mention the previous owner. He was a patient of mine with financial troubles. He lost millions when the stock market crashed in 2008. His son found him in the garage lying next to his Rolls Royce with the motor running and the garage door closed. The rest is history. I went to the funeral and haven't spoken to his family since. That was many months ago."

"Oh my! That's terrible," mentioned Maria.

"I remember reading about that online. I know who it was now," said Samantha.

After brunch the close friends went to the open house near the University. The home was much smaller than the others. It had hard wood floors, 4 bedrooms, 3 bathrooms, and a balcony off the master bedroom. There was a beautiful rose garden with a fountain. This home was built in the 1930's and has been remodeled a couple of times but still had an old feel to it. There were black and white photos on the walls, a gun rack over the fire place, lace curtains, and antique furniture. The price was $900,000.

"Sam, come look at the fountain with me," suggested Juan. He wanted to speak with her alone.

"What's up?"

"Are you and Jay exclusive? Sorry. It's none of my business but I heard him on the phone and--- He was probably talking to his sister or maybe his brother. I shouldn't say anything."

"Jay's an only child."

"The conversation sounded suspicious. He said, 'I miss you too,' as if he's involved with someone else. I just don't want you to get hurt. It could be nothing. I'm sorry."

"Don't be sorry. You're just looking out for me. I appreciate it. I'll be cautious," said Samantha.

Maria walked towards them. "So, what do you think about this place? It has an old feel to it. I'm not that crazy about it."

"I like it but it doesn't suit the two of you. You're a modern couple and you need a modern home," said Samantha.

"I agree. Let's get out of here," said Juan.

The friends went back to The Ritz Carlton and gathered at the pool before taking a walk on the beach. Juan had to leave soon to drive to Los Angeles and Melanie and Jay both had red-eye flights to catch before midnight. Jay's phone rang on the way to the beach. Of course, it was Stacey asking about his flight. They've only known each other a short time and she was clinging to Jay like a parasite. Stacey was a gold digger and knew Jay had money and good looks. She didn't care if he had a girlfriend. She figured long distance relationships didn't work and knew Jay would get tired of flying across the country. Jay veered off toward a sand dune to talk to her.

"Who's going to find the first sand dollar?" asked Margaret.

"That sounds like a great name for my jewelry store. I'll check tomorrow to see if the name is taken or not," said Maria.

"It sounds unique. It probably isn't taken," said Melanie.

Jay got off the phone. "That was work. Sorry honey." He held Samantha's hand and continued to walk. "Hey Mel, would you like to share a cab to the airport tonight?"

"That sounds good. Our flights leave around the same time."

"I should take you back to my place soon so you can pack your things," said Samantha.

"Found one!" said Margaret as she handed the sand dollar to Maria. "It's yours for good luck."

"Thank you, Margaret. That's so sweet."

Maria and Juan went to the valet to retrieve Juan's convertible and say goodbye. They kissed passionately before Juan got in the car. He drove to the highway and headed South to Los Angeles while listening to his favorite 1980's music.

Margaret went home to do chores and chew some Nicorette Gum and Jay packed his things to go back to the hotel to meet up with Melanie. Samantha dropped Jay off and he only gave her a kiss on the cheek and got out of the car in a hurry. She drove off while looking in the rear-view mirror and Jay didn't look at her; only at his phone.

Melanie and Jay arrived at the airport and the cab driver put Melanie's Gucci luggage on the curb while Jay got his own bag. Jay paid the driver and gave him a nice tip.

"What a gentleman. Thank you. I can pay the sky cap."

"If you must."

The two of them went through security and proceeded to the monitors.

"It looks like both of our flights are delayed. It's a good thing we are both flying American Airlines," said Jay.

"Why is that?"

"I belong to the Elite American Club. Come with me. I'll buy you a drink."

"I like the sound of that."

They walked up to the foggy glass doors and Jay swiped his card to open the doors. Melanie had only been in one of these places years ago with her former husband and you had to be a millionaire to be a member. The club was plush and modern with a touch of 1960's chic. A place where James Bond would order a martini before going on his next mission. It even had a sunken-in den with a stainless-steel fireplace with velvet sofas and a 75-inch flat screen TV featuring sports. Many passengers were on their cell phones but many still had Black Berry's considering it was 2010 and not everyone owned a smart phone. The view of the runway was the best part. You can see every plane take off and land. Jay and Melanie walked over to the bar.

"Hello stranger," said the bartender with big breasts and porcelain white teeth.

"Hello Ginger. This is my friend Melanie. Our flights are delayed and we would love some drinks."

"Flights?" Ginger thought they were flying together.

"Yes. I'm flying home to NY and Melanie is flying home to Vegas. We were here visiting friends."

"Jay's girlfriend lives here in Santa Barbara and she's also my best friend from college," said Melanie in a snappy tone. Jay gave Melanie a dirty look.

"That's wonderful Jay. I didn't know you were attached. She's a lucky lady." Ginger walked away to cash out a client.

"I don't usually talk about my personal life to Ginger."

"Yes, I can see that. I know her type. I used to work in a club, remember? She undressed you with her eyes and if I wasn't here, she would probably follow you to NY and fuck your brains out." Melanie had street smarts and knew women who came from nothing. She is Las Vegas high society and can play any part.

"Excuse me! You aren't allowed to talk that way. This is a prestigious club and besides, Ginger isn't like that anymore."

Melanie rolled her eyes. "Great. I hope I don't have to worry about you now."

"I used to be a player but now that I'm older I'm ready to settle down so you can calm down already."

Melanie stared at his face long and hard while Ginger brought the drinks. She decided to change the subject and talked to Jay about his restaurant and how he became successful. Jay talked about how he grew up an only child in a wealthy family. His father worked on Wall Street as a banker and his mother a tennis instructor at a country club. Both his parents are deceased. They passed away three months apart right after Jay graduated from NYU. His father died from complications from Diabetes and his mother died three months after that from a heart attack. Rumor has it she died of a broken heart but also could not tolerate his indiscretions when he was alive. There was a serious cheating scandal back in the day. Melanie spoke of her past and how she married a wealthy man for his money and knew he was terminally ill. Melanie is a millionaire now and can buy her own businesses if she so desires. Jay has less income but they both travel first class. They enjoyed the next two hours together and hugged good-bye in the terminal and went their separate ways to catch their flights.

CHAPTER 9

It was a beautiful and crisp morning in Santa Barbara with the wind blowing and the palm trees swaying side to side. Maria closed the sliding glass door of the balcony and slipped on her pumps and went down to the front desk to check out of the hotel. Samantha was picking her up to look at the vacant shop on State Street.

"You picked the perfect day to go back home. I work today so I can buy you breakfast at the airport," said Samantha as she popped the trunk for Maria.

"This is my home now, not Dallas."

"Good to hear that. You need to kiss Texas goodbye. Your life is here now. Not to change the subject but, you know, if you don't fall in love with this shop in the first five minutes it won't be a done-deal."

"I know I will love it. My heart was racing when I first saw it," said Maria.

Needless to say, it was a done-deal in the first four minutes. Maria shook hands with the realtor and took the paper work with her and called Juan with the great news. Juan was very happy and they talked about the home overlooking the mission. They wanted to see it one more time before making a deposit.

"Did you know I spoke to Dr. King and she updated the drink menu at Paradise Café? She has a drink called 'JACK'S COSMO'. It's a Cosmopolitan Martini with a splash of Pomegranate juice. It is superb. I wish you were able to taste it because you know I can't. It's a hot item."

"I'll try one when I get to Santa Barbara."

"I have to run babe. I'll see you this weekend. I love you."

"I love you too."

"The two of you are so sweet," said Samantha as she put her key card in the slot to open the gate at the airport.

It was 1am and wet in New York City. You can hear the tires splashing in the street puddles from the taxies and Jay pulled the door shut and locked his restaurant. Stacey walked up the sidewalk wearing a fur coat, fishnet stockings, and black patent leather stilettos. Jay was not in the mood for drama. "What's going on Stacey? I'm pretty beat. I just want to get home and relax alone."

"I was worried. You didn't return my calls. Were you busy?"

"Very busy. You don't work here anymore. I already gave you a letter of reference for your next job."

"I know. I just wanted to see you one last time. May I buy you a drink?" she asked as she opened her coat so Jay can see her lingerie. She was wearing a black lace bra with matching garter belt and panties. Her white smooth stomach was exposed with a crystal stud in her belly button.

"Look Stacey, I have a girlfriend. I don't want to be fucking around anymore. She means a lot to me."

Stacey put his hand inside her coat so he can feel her smooth skin. She moved his hand down to her panties so he can feel the warm lace.

"If she means that much to you then why are you living on opposite sides of the country? I want to please you one last time and then I'll leave you alone. I promise. I've never met a man like you before and I want to do things to you that no other woman can do."

"It's starting to rain again," said Jay as he moved his hand to her breast and up to her cheek to kiss her lips. His Town Car pulled around and he told her to get in. "We can't make a habit of this. This is the last time, ok?"

"Whatever you say." They kissed and went straight to his penthouse.

Jay and Stacey finally arrived after ten minutes of foreplay in the back of his Town Car. The doorman opened the brass door and they caught the elevator and did more kissing. She unzipped his pants and the elevator door opened to his penthouse.

"Shouldn't we have a drink first?"

"Ok, I'll turn on the fireplace," said Stacey as she moved the white shag carpet further away from the fireplace.

"You don't need to move that. Those aren't real flames. It's not a real fire. It's for ambiance."

"That's right. I forgot."

Jay handed her a scotch on the rocks and went into the bathroom. Stacey pulled a small camera out of her coat pocket and set it on the mantel between the décor so it couldn't be seen in the dark. She looked into the lens and blew a kiss and winked. This was Stacey's moment to be a star. She continued to look into the lens as she dipped her finger into her scotch and then put her finger in her mouth seductively. Jay came out of the bathroom in his silk boxers.

"Why don't you take off your pumps and coat and stay a while."

"That sounds like a plan. I'll need help with my coat."

After Jay and Stacey were done with their escapade Stacey made sure to go through Jay's cell phone to see if Samantha's email address was listed under his contacts. Sure enough it was and she wrote it down and put the camera back in her coat pocket while Jay was in the bathroom. Stacey poured two more drinks and Jay called his driver to come pick up Stacey in thirty minutes. They kissed passionately before she left and the elevator door closed. He was slightly relieved. Jay looked in the mirror and finished his drink. It took him a few minutes to realize what he had done. He felt ashamed. Little did he know, the sex was recorded. He didn't like the smell of Stacey's perfume on his robe so he immediately threw it in the hamper and went to take a shower. The housekeeper will take care of his laundry tomorrow.

A few days had gone by and Maria arrived in Santa Barbara in her blue Pontiac. She was happy to be out of Texas and staying at The Ritz Carlton with Juan until their home was ready to move in. Samantha was busy working and had a 24-hour layover in Las Vegas and spent it with Melanie in her beautiful home. It was almost Autumn and the weather was perfect in Las Vegas. It usually cools down in the Fall and gets extremely warm in late Spring when Melanie spends five months at Margaret's beach house every year.

"Should we stay in or go out? You're probably beat from working so let's spend time in the hot tub and order Chinese."

"You took the words right out of my mouth, girl." Samantha smiled.

"Have you heard from Jay?"

No. I sent him a text yesterday but he didn't respond. He's been acting strange lately. When he was visiting me, he was cold and distant. That's not like him. He wanted to be exclusive but I don't think he wants to commit. His actions say he doesn't want a relationship."

"I got that impression at the airport also. He doesn't act like a man in a relationship. His past is catching up with him and he has skeletons in his closet. He was flirtatious with the bartender at the Elite American Club and he admitted to a fling with her in the past. Also, Juan mentioned something about him at their golf game. He was texting and taking calls from a woman named Stacey. It could have been work related but I doubt it."

"Juan mentioned that to me also and told me to be cautious. Maybe he is a *bad-boy* after all."

Maria was drinking cheap AA coffee with a shortbread cookie and talking with others at the university. Dr. King was able to notify her of all of the meetings before scheduling their therapy sessions. She just received a text from Juan and she was anxious to see him after almost two weeks. They met at Paradise Café for dinner and she told him how great the meeting was and she found a new sponsor. They each got on their phones to call their close friends, Margaret, Melanie, Samantha, and Jay. Of course, Jay didn't pick up so Juan sent him a text and they finished their dinner. They talked with the staff and had a wonderful time before going back to The Ritz.

Maria took a long hot bath and relaxed with a cup of tea. Juan came into the bathroom while Maria was finishing up.

"We can do a walk-through on the house tomorrow and sign the papers. Does that sound like a plan?" asked Juan.

"It sounds wonderful."

"You aren't homesick, are you?"

"I don't miss Dallas. There was nothing for me there. I basically left with the clothes on my back. I have a suitcase and two small boxes in the back seat of my car with knick-knacks that Jack gave me over the years."

"I think it will hit you once we move into the house. You will go through a few days of culture shock."

The two of them stayed in the rest of the night and watched a movie while Juan rubbed Maria's feet before they both fell asleep.

Maria woke up early to use the gym and called Dr. King to make an appointment for therapy. Samantha had called and said she was on her way home and couldn't wait to see her and Juan. There was still no word from Jay and Samantha decided to e-mail him when she arrived home.

Juan woke up and looked at his schedule. He didn't have a gig until next week and he didn't have to go to L.A. until next month. This gave him plenty of time to shop for furniture with Maria. Maria came back from the gym and saw Juan in the shower through the transparent door.

"Babe, do you want to get breakfast?"

"Sure. What's on the agenda today?" asked Juan.

"Besides the walk-through?"

"Yeah. Do you want to look at furniture?"

"Ok. Samantha might come with us. She's concerned about Jay. She hasn't heard from him and he won't return her text messages. It's been almost two weeks."

"Something's not right with that guy. I think he's screwing around. You know, cheating and what not. He was flirting a lot with women on the course when we were golfing," Juan said as he rinsed off.

"You might be right."

Samantha landed at the Santa Barbara Airport and grabbed a coffee in the terminal before driving home. When she arrived home, she put on comfortable clothes and spent a few minutes with Margaret.

"I like this 80's music you're playing," said Samantha.

"I love it. I never get tired of it. How was work and Vegas?"

"I was only there for one night and I stayed with Melanie."

"Have you heard from lover-boy?"

"Not one word. I'm getting ready to email him to see where we stand. I feel like I'm in limbo. I don't want to be in an unstable relationship."

"You should express that in the email. You never know, he may want to see other people because of the distance and all."

"You might be right."

Samantha went back home and opened her laptop to read her emails. There was an email from a woman named Stacey. She doesn't know anyone by that name and thinks its spam and is afraid to open it thinking it will cause a virus but her computer is protected so she went ahead and opened it.

'Your boyfriend is amazing. Click here.'

She couldn't believe her eyes. It was a sex video of some woman and Jay. Samantha's heart stopped for a few seconds while she caught her breath. She continued to watch in shock and couldn't even cry. The tears wouldn't flow. It felt like she was hit by a bus and couldn't move. Her hand was on the mouse but she couldn't feel it. She took a deep breath and closed the laptop. She went to the kitchen and opened her freezer and poured herself a glass of cold vodka. She went to the bedroom and sat on the foot of her bed drinking and staring at the wall. She had her answer. Samantha was no longer in limbo.

Maria tried calling Samantha but it went straight to voicemail.

"Honey, Samantha's not picking up her phone. Maybe her flight was delayed and she hasn't come home yet. We'll have to shop by ourselves."

"Ok, you can call her tonight," said Juan.

Melanie texted Samantha and she didn't get a response and figured she was napping. Margaret did the same.

Samantha woke up to find mascara stains on her pillow. She looked at her phone and realized she had slept 11 hours and three people had texted. Her head hurt so she went to the bathroom to take a strong pain pill. She returned the texts and also called Melanie.

"Hi. I'm glad you are still awake. I slept 11 hours."

'Are you feeling alright? Maybe its jetlag.'

"No. It looks like Jay is being unfaithful. He's seeing another woman and she emailed me a video of the two of them having sex!"

'What? Who does that shit? That is fucked up! What kind of bitch does this? Are you sure it's not an old video from before you met?'

"I don't know. Do you want me to send it to you?"

'Yes! I want to see this ass hole in action. Maybe I can figure out how recent it is. Have you confronted him?'

"No. Should I?"

'You should email him since he's not returning your texts. Send me the link and I will call you in the morning.'

"Ok. I'll talk to you tomorrow."

Samantha forwarded the email she received from Stacey and sent it to Jay and wrote: *I'm glad you are having a good time. WE ARE OVER!!'*

CHAPTER 10

The sky was still cloudy from the autumn rain and the maple leaves stuck to the sidewalk. It was a breezy 65 degrees outside the Paradise Café but the ladies decided to have their Pumpkin Spice Latte's inside. Samantha and Maria just came from their therapy sessions with Dr. King and Margaret met them shortly after. Maria was doing well with the grieving process but Samantha was still struggling with her issues with Jay. She had blocked him from her cell phone so he can't call or text but she has received countless emails and flowers apologizing for the incident. It had been six weeks since receiving the traumatic email from Stacey, the whore, and it wasn't getting much easier. Tomorrow was Halloween and Juan and Maria were throwing a nice dinner party at their new mansion. It will be a House Warming/ Halloween party with 25 of their closest friends. The party will be catered so there wasn't much to do except decorate which the girls will be doing today.

"Are you still getting emails from Jay?" asked Maria.

"Yes, but not as often. Maybe he'll stop eventually. They go directly to junk mail anyway and I will block him soon. I can put this behind me."

"What about the medication you are taking? Do you still need it? asked Margaret.

"I only take one pill before bed. I probably won't fill the prescription. It doesn't seem necessary. I just need a rebound man to take my mind off of Jay and I'll be good to go."

"You'll find a nice man at the Halloween Party," said Maria as she finished her latte.

The smell of primrose filled the air outside and the ladies went off to decorate Maria's home. After two hours of decorating the ladies ordered a pizza and talked about good times.

"Does Melanie fly in tonight or tomorrow?" asked Margaret.

"She flies in tomorrow morning and she is bringing a male friend with her. I think she is trying to set me up with him. Some guy that owns the club where she used to dance at. His name is Bruno. A real go-getter from Jersey," replied Samantha.

"Sounds fun. Is anyone dressing up tomorrow? It is optional. I'm setting the stereo on satellite radio. Should we play smooth jazz or soft rock?" asked Maria.

"I'm dressing up as a fancy witch and the music is up to you. I'm just looking forward to the deviled eggs. Melanie is wearing her old bunny costume," replied Samantha.

"I'm surprised she can still fit in that thing," said Margaret.

"I'm dressing as a cat and Juan will be a vampire," said Maria.

The ladies continued to eat pizza with the cheese sticking to the roof of their mouths.

Samantha woke up to another email from Jay and she finally decided to respond with a spleenful message so he would leave her alone for a while. She smelled the coffee coming from Margaret's house and invited Samantha over for Eggs Benedict.

"Happy Halloween. What are you dressing up as?" asked Samantha.

"I decided to be a cat. It's pretty simple. Hey, I think I'm over the hump now. I haven't had a cigarette in six weeks and I'm no longer on the patch."

"That's fantastic Margaret! We have to celebrate. Do you think there will be booze at the party? You know, Maria's in AA."

"I'm sure there will be. She's okay with people drinking as long as she doesn't touch the stuff. Juan drinks occasionally just not around her."

"I don't care about dieting today. I'm eating everything."

"Good for you. There's going to be a full moon tonight."

Melanie and Bruno arrived at Maria's home and parked across the street. The house was lit up beautifully and there were lit jack-o-lanterns on each step of the walk way leading up to the door. Bruno decided to go as a Yankees Baseball player. He wore the striped uniform and baseball cap with his pants tucked into his socks and Melanie was in her pink bunny costume with pink stiletto heels. She looked like she belonged back at the Playboy Mansion. Juan opened the door and Maria snapped a picture.

"Welcome to our haunted house," said Juan in a Dracula voice.

"It doesn't look very haunted. It's all lit up and pretty," replied Bruno in his New Jersey accent.

"Oh my God! Look at all the decorations. This house is gorgeous Maria," said Melanie.

"Thank you. Come and meet Juan's friends."

Dr. King showed up wearing an orange dress but couldn't stay long. She had to get back to Paradise Café. Everyone was having a great time and Bruno and Samantha were getting to know one another. The swimming pool was lit up with orange candles floating on lily pads. Maria and Samantha went to the fence to enjoy the view.

"This morning I got the binoculars out and I could see Jack's plot from here."

"Really? That is so cool. You are so lucky to live here."

"I know. I count my blessings every day. How are you holding up? You look like you lost some weight."

"I'm actually doing better. Today is the first day I've felt well since the incident and I'm getting my appetite back. Jay sent me an email and I responded. I told him to leave me alone for a while so I can think. I'll have to forgive him eventually so I can move on with my life."

"Do you think you can date him again?"

"I doubt it but, never say 'never'."

Inside the house people were dressed in costumes and gathering around the kitchen and bar and enjoying the music and food. The bar contained five barstools and behind the bar there were four glass shelves with wine and shot glasses. On the second shelf was a black and white photo of Jack inside a brass frame with a sand dollar glued to the side. It was a perfect place for the photo since Jack was a bartender.

Juan had only bought the basic liquor and any unused portion will be donated to Paradise Café. Juan took Maria's alcoholism very seriously and didn't want any alcohol in the house; not even a bottle of cold medicine. Maria couldn't believe how much Juan loved and cared for her. Her life seemed so perfect. The new home, the new jewelry store, money in the bank, great friends, a wonderful relationship, etc. Maria had a hard life up until Jack passed away. If it wasn't for Jack's passing, she wouldn't have this life. She would still be struggling in Texas trying to make ends meet.

Bruno had a Gray Goose Martini in one hand and a pretzel in the other. He noticed the picture of Jack behind the bar.

"What is it?" asked Melanie.

"I know that guy. Seriously. I've seen him in the club. What's his name?"

"Jack Turner. He used to tend bar at Paradise Café here in Santa Barbara. He's Maria's brother."

"Are you kidding me? He's a drug dealer. I chased him out of the club last year after I caught him selling cocaine to one of my girls. I fired her after that. I run a clean business. No funny stuff."

"Well, you won't be seeing him anymore. He was killed several months ago and why do you call them *your girls*? They aren't whores and you're not a pimp."

"Excuse me! I say that because they are like family. I treat them like they are my daughters. Trust me; I'm old enough to be their father. Half of them are in law school. So, how did the creep die? Was it an angry husband or a deal gone wrong?"

"I want to say it was a deal gone wrong. His car went over a cliff and the cops found a briefcase full of cocaine in his car. No one ever suspected he was a dealer. Not even Maria. She took it hard and is still in therapy for it," said Melanie as she took a sip of her Cosmopolitan.

Melanie decided to mingle and Bruno went outside to be near Samantha and Maria. He passed by a beautifully lit fountain.

"Hey, can I throw money in this thing? All I have are casino chips," laughed Bruno. He was being cocky.

"Sure, anything will do. The pool man will keep the chips. He's the guy that cleans the fountain," replied Maria.

"You have a lovely home, Maria. You and Juan have done very well for yourselves," Bruno said in his New Jersey accent.

"Thank you so much. I better get inside and make the rounds. I'll leave the two of you to your conversation. Let me know if you need more drinks."

"Thank you, sweetie," said Samantha.

Bruno and Samantha got to know each other over the next 45 minutes. She spoke of Jay and her job and he spoke of his night club and where he is from and his connections to important men. He didn't mention organized crime but she got the hint. He moved to Las Vegas to get away from that lifestyle but when your uncle is doing time for being a crime boss it stays with you. Italians are very loyal people and they have each other's back. Samantha understood and didn't judge. Samantha is also loyal. Her best friend used to be an exotic dancer before she married the millionaire hotel mogul. Melanie and Bruno are close friends and sometimes she helps out at the club and sometimes Bruno helps with her charity work. Melanie runs the Humane Society in Vegas and donates her time at the school for Autism. She always wanted children of her own and this makes up for it. She still speaks to her step children who are almost her age. Bruno has no children.

It was close to 1:00 am and the party was dwindling down to just a few people. The close friends sat around the fire pit outside and exchanged stories while the full moon cast a shadow through the palm trees.

Morning broke through the drapes in the bedroom and Juan woke up without the alarm. It was 8:30 am so he started a pot of coffee, took a fast shower, and put the bottles of liquor in the trunk of his car. He called Paradise Café to make sure someone would let him in. He put his coffee in a travel mug and off he went.

Melanie and Bruno had a 2-bedroom suite at The Ritz Carlton. Bruno went to use the gym and Melanie went to swim laps before calling Samantha for brunch. Juan made plans to golf with Bruno and Maria decided to take a walk on the beach with Margaret. It seemed everyone was paired off to do what made them happy. Surprisingly, Bruno played very well at golf and Juan enjoyed the challenge. It was a close game. Bruno was interested in going to Maria's jewelry store to look at necklaces. They both showered at the hotel and Juan called Maria to see if there was time before the store closed. Maria thought it would be best for Bruno to shop after hours so she can give him special service.

It was 3:30pm and Samantha and Melanie had switched from Mimosa's to Mojito's by the pool.

"So, what do you think about Bruno? He seems to be attracted to you."

"Are you sure that's not his Italian charm? He smells nice and I like his pinky ring. He's like a big teddy bear."

"He protects the ladies at the club. There is no funny business. He's a straight shooter and he has money," said Melanie as she pulled the mint leaf out of her drink.

"We talked last night and he knows about Jay. He knows I'm confused. I don't even know if I'm done with Jay. He still wants me back."

"I know he does. You're a good catch. He's not ready to let you go. I did send an email to Stacey."

"What for? She's a whore!"

"I know. I basically said it was immature to do what she did and that someday she should apologize. I was polite to her but I don't expect a response."

"You won't get one. She needs to grow up."

"Bruno just texted me about dinner at Paradise Café after shopping at the jewelry store."

"Are we shopping?" asked Samantha.

"Apparently, Bruno is in the mood to Christmas shop."

"He likes to shop? I like him better already."

Samantha and Melanie realized they were not sober enough to drive so they had to take a taxi to Sand Dollar Jewelry Store to meet everyone. Bruno had his eye on the sand dollar necklaces made out of 14K gold. They were $150 a piece and he bought ten of them for the ladies at the club. Melanie bought a pearl necklace and Samantha bought a sterling silver bracelet. They all received the 25% friends and family discount. This made Maria very happy. She wasn't expecting this kind of sale today. Paradise Café was only three doors down so they were able to walk to have dinner.

The next morning everyone went their separate ways. Bruno and Melanie flew back to Vegas, Samantha went to work and flew to

Chicago, Juan had a meeting in Los Angeles, Maria had inventory at the jewelry store, and Margaret was remodeling her guest room.

Chicago was known for its wind and it was no joke. There was so much turbulence most of the flight crew felt nauseated when they landed. After the passengers finally left the plane Samantha was able to go to the Sky Club for ginger ale and Tylenol. She had a 2-hour layover before going to JFK and opened her laptop to browse and shop and check email. There was nothing from Jay and that surprised her. Was this a sign they were done or is he giving her space at her request? This made her miss him and her head was in a fog. She signed out of her email and continued to browse for apparel. She noticed a pilot looking her way and pretended not to notice. Samantha uncrossed her legs and crossed them again the other way. She found herself on a jewelry website looking at rings. All she had was a gold pinky ring on her right hand that her mother gave her years ago. If she wanted something fancy all she had to do was fly to Las Vegas and go through Melanie's jewelry closet and borrow something. Also, Maria owns a jewelry store and she can buy a ring to match the bracelet she bought from her.

Samantha checked her agenda and saw she was working First Class on her next flight. She closed her laptop and headed towards the ladies' room to freshen up. She checked her makeup and put on her Cotton Candy Pink lipstick and spritzed some Coco Chanel. While leaving the ladies room she noticed three young men dressed like rock stars walking towards the gate. They were dressed in tight skinny jeans, bright shirts, jet black hair, and guy liner. The man in the middle was wearing green skinny jeans and a guitar case on his back. His hair was spiked and he had the latest 2010 iPod on his hip with ear buds in his ears. This reminded Samantha of a great time in the past with Melanie in the 1980's. For a moment she was in a *Duran* time warp. Mr. Green Pants turned around to look for a recycling bin for his soda can and Samantha noticed his bright green eyes that matched his pants. Everything was moving in slow motion as though she was in a music video. She kept waiting for the fog from the dry ice to appear from behind the musicians. Mr. Green Pants dropped his can into the bin and winked at Samantha. She smiled and turned around slowly and for a moment she was in a happy place and this took her mind off of Jay. She knew she still had her good looks to carry her through the day.

The doors on the plane were shut and the plane proceeded to the runway as Samantha went over the safety procedures. The musicians were on her left and three business men on her right. The flight was only half full and this made for an easy work day as the plane was ready for takeoff.

The plane reached a comfortable altitude and the *fasten seat belt sign* stayed on as the pilot spoke on the intercom. Samantha had only three drink orders to take. Mr. Green Pants sat in front of the other two musicians with a vacant seat to his right. He ordered a Grey Goose and Seven and smiled his nice white teeth at Samantha. He read her gold name tag and realized who she was.

"You don't remember me, do you?" asked the sexy rock star. Samantha thought to herself as her palms began to sweat. '*He either thinks I'm a groupie or I had a one-night-stand with this guy last century and he's coming back to haunt me.*'

"Excuse me? You must think I'm someone else but I'm flattered anyway."

"It's me, Billy. Billy Taylor. I was a friend of Jack's. I sang at his funeral."

He spoke with a British accent and Samantha's eyes opened wide. "Oh my God! I didn't recognize you! I'm so happy to see you! I thought you were just flirting with me."

"I was dressed more conservative the last time you saw me."

Samantha excused herself to take other orders and they talked some more before she brought out the in-flight meals. It was a coincidence that all four of them were staying at The Hyatt Hotel in Times Square in NYC one block away from Jay's restaurant. Billy and the Band had a limo waiting for them at JFK airport and asked Samantha to join them.

When they landed paparazzi were waiting for them in baggage claim. Samantha was stunned and Billy grabbed her hand so he wouldn't lose her. Flashes were going off in her face so she put her left hand up with her palm out to guard her face. Security threw out everyone that wasn't a passenger so they could get their luggage and proceed to the limo. More flashes went off before closing the car door. Before Billy could roll up the window a photographer yelled out. "Billy! Is this your new girlfriend? What is her name? Billy!!"

Samantha didn't know if knowing Billy should be shared with her colleagues when she sees them at the end of the week. They will be asking questions and who knows which magazine the photos will end up. All she could do was smile; something she hasn't done in a while. She hadn't thought about Jay since she ran into Billy and the Band in Chicago. Billy's publicist was waiting for him at the hotel with penthouse key cards.

"Do you have a gig tonight?" asked Samantha.

"No, tomorrow and the next five nights at Madison Square Garden. Are you available? What is your schedule like?"

"I don't have to be in California until the end of the week. I really need to get a room and relax."

"Here's a room key for you. You'll be across the hall," said Billy as the four of them slipped into the service elevator with two huge body guards.

"I can't accept this."

"You don't have a choice now. It's a done deal. When will you be hungry? Do you have plans?"

"No plans except a long hot bubble bath. I'll be hungry in about two hours."

"Would you like a martini to go with that bubble bath?"

"I wouldn't mind that."

Samantha went to her suite to put her luggage down and check it out and then went over to Billy's suite to get a martini. They talked for a few minutes while Billy made a nice Cosmopolitan for her to take back to the room.

Samantha went back to take a long hot bath and couldn't stop smiling. She promised to be back in two hours with no makeup and just a pair of sweats. Billy was going to order pizza and the other two boys were going out.

Jay was in his New York restaurant sitting at the end of the bar having his usual Scotch when he noticed a tabloid TV show featuring Billy and the Band and their upcoming concert at Madison Square Garden. The paparazzi filmed the mob scene at the airport and The Hyatt Regency Hotel and Jay was able to see Samantha in the coverage. Billy wasn't able to protect her from the cameras after all. Jay stood up and stared at the TV and asked the bartender to turn up the volume. He couldn't believe Samantha was in town. He wanted to see her. He missed her so much. Jay finished his drink and went over to the Hyatt four blocks down. He paced in the lobby before texting Samantha. Samantha finished her bath and enjoyed the nice suite before going to Billy's room. Jay picked up a magazine and went to the hotel bar for a drink and appetizer. He didn't know if Samantha would respond so he had another drink to calm his nerves before texting her. Sports played on the bar TV while Jay stirred his ice cubes in his glass and turned to glance at the lobby and noticed a young man in his late twenties with body guards checking in. This was either Josh Groban or someone who looked similar. Samantha knocked on Billy's door and they began to enjoy their casual evening.

"I saw beautiful pictures of Juan and Maria's new home on Facebook. I wish I could've gone to the Halloween party but I was on tour. I still am, actually. How is everyone else doing? How is Jay? He works down the street you know." Billy poured a light beer into a glass.

"Jay and I are on a little break for now."

"Oh, tell me what happened; if you want. I don't want to pry."

Samantha's phone vibrated. Jay finally had the nerve to text.

'I saw you on TV. I am in the lobby of The Hyatt. Are you here?'

"Speak of the devil. He just texted me."

'I'm eating dinner. I'll call you later.'

Jay was just happy to get a response so he paid his bill and walked back to his restaurant in the rain with no umbrella.

Samantha and Billy had a great time catching up and eating pizza for two hours before turning in for the night. Billy kissed Samantha on the cheek and wished her pleasant dreams. "I'll see you tomorrow night at the concert," said Billy.

"I wouldn't miss it."

Samantha went to her room and immediately called Jay. She left the hotel and Jay left his restaurant. It began to rain harder but she didn't care. She looked at the Empire State Building lit up in the distance. Her heart began to beat faster as she saw a man approaching her way. She stopped. Her sneakers were soaked and her feet felt like lead. It was Jay. He walked slowly towards her. A cab drove by and splashed him but he was already soaked. Jay was only a few feet away and couldn't move. All they could do was stare at each other as Jay began to smile and Samantha smiled back.

CHAPTER 11

Samantha woke up at 11:00 am to her vibrating cell phone. It was Melanie so she let it go to voicemail until she was fully awake. She turned to her left and put her arm around Jay's naked body and realized she had forgiven him and put things in the past. He had given her a wonderful night of passion and he truly loved her and wanted to be a serious man in her life. Samantha went to the bathroom and used the phone in there to order room service. She stayed in the bathroom to retrieve her voicemail. Melanie had seen her on TV and wanted to know what was happening so she called her back and explained everything before she heard the doorbell. "Room service."

"This place has a doorbell?" Samantha opened the door.

"Good morning Ms. Kerry."

"Please come in." She kissed Jay on the cheek to wake him up and she ended her call with Melanie while the attendant set up the breakfast table. He left three minutes later and Jay got out of bed and Samantha sat at the table in her white terry cloth robe the hotel had provided for her. The land line rang while she poured the coffee. "Hello?"

"Are you awake?" asked Billy.

"Yes. I'm eating breakfast and I slept well," said Samantha with a smile. Jay put on a t-shirt and his red silk boxers.

"I have two back stage passes for the concert tonight. Do you know anyone that would like to go with you?"

"Yes. I will round someone up. May I call you this afternoon after your rehearsal?"

"Yes. We'll have a snack in the room. We'll talk then. Good bye gorgeous."

"Bye." Samantha smiled and looked at Jay. "That was Billy. He has two back stage passes for tonight. Are you available?"

"I think I can manage. Do we need to shop for an outfit for you?"

"Oh my God, yes! I don't have proper attire."

"Then it's a date. We'll shower and go to Macy's," said Jay.

"Will you also buy a smoothie for me afterward?"

"Of course. Will that be your lunch?" Jay asked jokingly.

After three hours of shopping Samantha received a text from Melanie.

'Are you free in a few days? Are you able to fly to Vegas or I'll come to you?'

'I'm working a flight to Miami and then I'll fly to Las Vegas on Sunday evening. Looking forward to it.'

'You R a slutty jetsetter. Lol.'

'Lol ☺'

Jay and Samantha walked down 5th Ave. with their smoothies and Macy's bags. It was 45 degrees and getting colder.

"We should be drinking hot coco not smoothies," said Jay. They found a bench to sit on so they can people-watch.

"New York always gets colder after they put up the Christmas decorations. It's part of the ambiance," said Samantha.

"Five more weeks until Christmas. The restaurant is getting booked up with holiday parties. Speaking of the restaurant, I do have to slip in and check on things. I know you want to get to the concert on time and you need to get ready so I'll have my driver take you to The Hyatt and I will meet you later."

"That sounds good."

Samantha made it back to the hotel room with shopping bags in tow. She called Billy's room to make sure he was there and went across the hall to knock on his door with her outfit in one bag.

"I ordered cheese and wine and room service will probably bring bread as well," Billy said as he tossed music sheets on the coffee table. The two other band members were in the other room singing and practicing their lyrics.

"I need to be honest with you."

"What's up babe?" asked Billy.

"Jay caught up with me last night and he stayed over. I feel awkward. I'll pay for the room."

"Don't be ridiculous. The record label is paying for everything. I'm glad you and Jay are getting along."

"I suppose. We'll have to talk some more before I can fully trust him again." Billy changed the subject as he sipped his wine.

"This is a great Merlot. I'll be very relaxed for my massage. A massage therapist will be here in an hour."

"Lucky you. May I show you the dress I bought? Actually, Jay bought it for me."

Jay got ready for the concert in Samantha's room and the limo was waiting downstairs.

"You have that parturient look on your face. Do you want to share?" Samantha said as she fastened a gold chain around Jay's neck.

"I would like to talk when we get back."

"About?"

"About us."

Samantha knew this was important and was curious about what he had to say. They proceeded to the concert and took the back stage entrance. There were six velvet red chairs for VIP's and they took the two in front. It was a packed house and Billy came out of his dressing room looking like the rock star he was. Cameras followed him to the stage and the crowd roared. Billy and the Band played two sets before taking a speech break where he talks to the audience and tells them what great fans they are. When the concert ended Billy came back stage and hugged everyone and had photos taken with Jay and Samantha. It was a night to remember and a true success.

Samantha and Jay made it back to the hotel and ordered room service. Jay took Samantha in his arms.

"I love you and I want this to work. I know it will be a while before you can trust me again. I promise it won't happen again. Please say you forgive me. I was an asshole."

"Yes you were but that's in the past. We can move forward. I love you too."

Samantha landed in Las Vegas the following evening and Melanie was waiting in her limo with a pink cocktail. Melanie got out and flagged her down.

"Oh my God! You look amazing!" said Melanie as they hugged. "Tell me everything about New York. I want to hear all of the juicy details and don't leave anything out."

"You look amazing too and what is in this drink? It's delicious."

"Just something to relax you. A pink grapefruit martini."

"Well, Jay and I are back together."

"This is good, right?"

"Yes. I'm happy about it and he promised to never cheat again."

"Bruno will be disappointed but I'm happy for you. If Jay fucks around again Bruno will mess him up."

"I figured that," said Samantha.

"Speaking of Bruno, he might stop by later."

"Sounds good."

Samantha received a text from Maria.

'When are you coming home? We miss you! We are planning Thanksgiving at Paradise Café.'

'I'm in Vegas. I'll be home the day after tomorrow. I miss you too!' replied Samantha.

When Melanie and Samantha arrived at the house Melanie took the luggage upstairs to the guest room and Samantha immediately took off her flight attendant uniform and put on a plush robe and collapsed on the bed. Melanie went downstairs to her computer to finish some work while Samantha slept. It wasn't long before Samantha fell into a deeper sleep with eidolons of Jack and Maria. Samantha always believed when you dream of the deceased they are actually saying 'hello' and checking on you. Jack was holding an open briefcase with a cooked turkey inside and Maria behind him wearing a black dress and a white wedding vail. Most dreams don't make any sense but she was willing to analyze this when she woke up.

Ninety minutes had gone by before Melanie's house phone rang. It was Bruno on his way with Chinese food. Samantha woke up and got in the shower. Melanie went upstairs to check on Samantha and entered the bedroom.

"Sam?"

"Yeah?"

"Bruno's on his way with Chinese food."

"Thank God. I'm starving."

"Do you want some chips so you won't pass out?" smiled Melanie.

"No. It will spoil my appetite. I love this auto-steam by the way."

Melanie always kept clean panties, body spray, deodorant, and items for any guest. Samantha stopped by at least twice a month to spend the night and Melanie loved to spoil her. Samantha put on a sports bra and pajamas. A clean face with no makeup was sufficient. Bruno would have to deal with it. He was downstairs already serving the food as he popped open a beer.

"Hey beautiful. I love a fresh face; very natural." Bruno kissed Samantha on the cheek and handed her a glass of wine.

"A man after my own heart. Food and wine. This is perfect," said Samantha.

"You are my two favorite ladies."

"You say that to all the girls," said Melanie as she took a bite of an eggroll.

"Speaking of girls, you know I do random locker inspections at the club. The girls know this. They sign a waiver when I hire them so they agree to it. It's for their own protection. I run a clean joint for their safety. Well, I had to fire a lady today for cocaine in her locker. I asked her where it came from and she said she bought it from Jack earlier this year. That doesn't make it okay. I gave her a week's pay and off she went. I gave it to one of my guys to dispose of it. No cops, no problem. I don't need them sniffing around my club and making everyone nervous."

"Don't mention this to Maria. It would just upset her," said Samantha.

"I don't know her well enough to say anything."

"I had a dream about Jack and Maria. Jack's spirit is going to be around for a while."

Three weeks went by and the Santa Barbara sky was bluer than the ocean as the three friends walked barefoot in the sand in the late morning before brunch. Maria, Juan, and Margaret talked about Thanksgiving even though it felt like summer. It was unusually warm out for November and it won't cool down until the end of the week. They enjoyed watching the surfers challenge the waves. Maria was always looking for sand dollars but didn't see any today but it didn't matter. She was in good company. They walked half a mile before turning around to Margaret's house for omelets and Danishes and then off to Paradise Café to meet Dr. King.

There were only a few customers at Paradise Café so it was a perfect time to discuss Thanksgiving and decorate. Maria and Margaret folded linen while Dr. King and Juan dusted and polished the stage. Juan went through half a bottle of Old English Polish making sure the piano looked nice and called the piano tuner to stop by later.

"Is anyone hungry? I can have the guys in back whip up something," asked Dr. King.

"Oh, no thank you. We just ate an hour ago," replied Maria.

"Is this event going to be 'reservation-only'?" asked Margaret.

"No, everyone is welcome. I put up flyers at the university and also left some in my waiting room at the office. Some of the students are not going home to their families until Christmas so we will be their family," replied Gwen King.

It was a cloudy Thanksgiving Day and 55 degrees in Santa Barbara. To most native Californians this is considered cold weather. Many people donned turtle neck sweaters or scarves before heading out. Maria and Juan slept in and Margaret woke up at 8am in her beach house with Melanie in the guest room. Margaret started the coffee and waited until 8:30 to call Samantha.

"Hi Sam. Are you awake?"

"I just woke up 10 minutes ago."

"Do you want to go for a jog or is Jay already here?"

"Jay's flight arrives at 11am and he's taking a cab so I don't have to get him. I'll finish my juice and come right over. Is Mel coming or is she still asleep?"

"I'll wake her. I'm sure she'll want to go."

"Alright. Bye."

Margaret woke up Melanie and put croissants in the oven for when they get back. Samantha showed up in her pink velour jogging suit while Melanie took a swig of Fiji water. The ladies jogged at a slow pace and noticed only two surfers in the water.

"If we find a sand dollar, that means Jack is jogging with us in spirit," said Margaret.

"I think he is always with us," replied Samantha.

On the way back they walked and Melanie found a sand dollar and she will give it to Maria this afternoon at Paradise Café.

Maria and Juan woke up in their beautiful home at 10:45 am. Maria read the news highlights on her laptop while Juan practiced a few songs on the grand piano with his coffee. Now that they are in the digital age there is no need for newspapers but Maria will occasionally pick one up on the way to the jewelry shop. Maria toasted a bagel and brought it to Juan and kissed his cheek while he was singing a number for today's venue. Maria took her coffee upstairs to shower and get ready.

Jay arrived at Samantha's house at 12:15 and she greeted him with a mimosa and crackers.

"I don't want you to spoil your appetite. We are eating around 2:30. Would you like some cheese? I have some brie left over," smiled Samantha.

"I'd love some. Thanks, beautiful."

Paradise Café looked stunning and festive with orange and white table cloths, silk autumn leaves, a candle on each table, and the aroma of pumpkin in the air. There were just a fair amount of guests, 60-65, and everyone knew each other. It was a casual buffet from salad to dessert and Juan was able to play a few songs in between courses. There were pictures being taken and people talking on their phones to loved ones back home. Melanie handed Maria the sand dollar and said, "Guess who's watching over you this holiday?" Maria replied with a smile and a tear in her eye. This was the happiest Maria had ever been. The close friends all posed for a picture on the stage and Gwen King took the photo. The ladies helped clean up and the men bussed the tables as the event came to a close. The bar was open for another 45 minutes and the bartender made Jack's martini for a select few. Maria talked about how busy her store was going to be tomorrow being Black Friday. It was exciting and Samantha offered to help since the boys were going golfing. Melanie and Margaret hadn't made plans but thought about finishing Melanie's bedroom. It was a wonderful holiday and the weekend was just beginning.

CHAPTER 12

Maria was putting the last finishing touches of lipstick to her coral colored lips when she felt the floor vibrate. She thought it might be a large truck driving down the street but the vibration grew stronger and her vanity table shook uncontrollably with makeup falling to the floor. She screamed loudly and Juan climbed up the stairs losing his balance and hitting the wall. Maria looked in the mirror and noticed the chandelier swaying side to side.

"Juan! Oh, my God!"

"Get under the table!" he yelled.

"What?!"

"Get under the table! Now!"

Juan couldn't fit with her so he just held her and covered her head with his arm and listened to things fall and crash downstairs. The rumbling slowly faded away and the lights went out. There was dead silence for 10 seconds until they heard a neighbor in the street yell.

"Hey! Is everyone all right?"

"Are you ok babe?" asked Juan.

"I think so."

"Stay here. I'll tell that guy we're fine."

"Are you kidding me? I'm going with you."

"I forgot. This is your first earthquake. Welcome to California."

"Funny."

"We should get our slippers in case of broken glass. We don't want to cut our feet."

They made it out of the house and all of the neighbors gathered in the street and tried to reach loved-ones on their cell phones. Most people couldn't get through. All circuits were busy and the cell towers couldn't handle so many calls at once. It was 7:35am and Maria looked around with a pale look on her face.

"The store! What if something happened to my store?"

"It's ok babe. You have insurance."

"But it's brand new!"

"We're safe. That's all that matters. So much for Black Friday."

A tall, lanky geek stood alone with his tablet checking the News.

"Hey guys! This was a 6.9 quake. Yeah, baby. Ha, ha!" He disappeared back into his house.

"Did you get through to the gang yet? I'm worried," asked Maria.

"Still trying."

Juan just received a text from Bruno. He was on his way to Sand Dollar Jewelers to check on the store and look for possible looters. The traffic lights weren't working so it took twice as long to get there.

"Bruno is on his way to your store to check things out," Juan said with a look of relief on his face.

"He doesn't have a key or know the alarm code."

"I'll text him the alarm code. He'll know how to get in. He has relatives in the Mob. I'm sure he's capable of getting in."

"Is it safe to go back inside? I want to call the girls."

"I think so. Let's go."

Lifeguards went up and down the beach with their vehicles and loud speakers trying to get surfers out of the water and everyone inland.

"Attention Please! Everyone out of the water immediately! There has been a tsunami warning. Please vacate the beach now! I repeat, vacate now!"

The surfers didn't feel a thing since being in the water. A jogger yelled,

"Get out of the water! There was an earthquake a few minutes ago!" The lifeguards put out a warning flag.

Melanie, Margaret, Jay, and Samantha were fine standing in the street with their robes on. Maria finally got through to the girls. "I'm glad you guys are alright. I'm still shaking. Only a couple of things broke and Bruno is checking on the store."

"We're still in the street and there has been a tsunami warning. If the epicenter was in the ocean, we are screwed," said Samantha in a nervous voice.

"I'm checking the laptop now. There hasn't been news yet except that it was a 6.9 quake."

"I better go and keep the cell lines open."

"I hear you. I'll talk to you later."

Maria swept the debris from the kitchen floor. Only two mugs and a jar of olives broke. The pictures and paintings were crooked but Juan wanted to wait to fix those. The electricity came back on followed by an after-shock of 4.9. Maria grabbed the kitchen counter top and watched the chandeliers sway from side to side. "Juan!"

"I'm on the staircase. It's just an after-shock. We'll get a few of those throughout the week."

"Ok."

Bruno called Juan and said the store was ok except for a large crack in the front window. He also found out the epicenter was in Montecito and not in the ocean so there was no need to panic. He texted the girls so they wouldn't worry about a tsunami and he patched up the crack with duct tape and went on his way to Paradise Café.

Bruno arrived at 8:40 am and Dr. Gwen King was already there sweeping the floor. He immediately hugged her and then checked on the grand piano. It was the most expensive thing in the place. The piano was fine. There were broken candle holders and bar glasses but the alcohol had not moved and Jack's picture did not shift at all.

"Jack must have been watching over this place. There's not much damage at all," said Dr. King as she emptied the dust pan into a trash barrel.

"I agree. How long has it been since Santa Barbara has been hit by a quake of this magnitude?"

"A good 20-25 years."

"Are you going to open your doors today?"

"Technically, you are not to open your doors for business until a building inspector comes to approve the premises. Anything over 6.0 requires that."

"That's good to know. I might know a guy," said Bruno with a sneaky look on his face.

"Why doesn't that surprise me?"

Meanwhile at the beach, everyone started getting ready to start their day. People were making coffee and watching the news unfold on TV. Travelers were able to drive out of Santa Barbara but there was no getting in to town. Flights were cancelled and some of the lanes on the Northbound interstate were closed due to falling boulders in Montecito. No drivers were injured but CHPs had a serious job on their hands getting drivers to merge. Juan drove Maria to the jewelry store to check on everything. The streets were empty and it looked like a ghost town. When they arrived, they noticed the front window patched up.

"We'll have to thank Bruno for this. Maybe we should get him a watch for Christmas," said Maria.

"What for? He has many watches."

"That figures."

Dr. King texted the friends and asked everyone to meet at Paradise Café in two hours for a safety briefing. Maria started a pot of coffee in the back and looked over some paper work. Juan was on his phone talking with his band members. Maria noticed a fancy Italian man on the sidewalk measuring the front window. He was wearing an expensive gray suit and black Prada shoes. She couldn't help but notice a shiny diamond on his right pinky finger and he also resembled Bruno with his black derby hat. She went outside to greet him.

"May I help you sir?"

"I'm Vinny. I'm here to fix your window."

"Are you with the insurance company?"

"I guess you can say that. Bruno sent me."

"Oh! I'm Maria."

He removed his derby. "The pleasure is all mine mam."

Juan got off the phone and greeted Vinny.

"It's ok Maria, go inside. Vinny is here to fix things."

Maria went inside and watched both of them. She couldn't believe the window was being repaired already the same day. She might be open for business today. It was now 10am. The two men walked over to a black Rolls Royce and shook hands before Vinny drove away. Juan came back inside. "Vinny and his crew will be back in an hour or so with a new window and the building inspector will sign off on the paperwork so you can reopen later today."

"Something tells me Vinny is not with the insurance company. He's some dark angel like Bruno."

"His rank is actually higher. I'll throw them some concert tickets to my show next month in Vegas and everything will be cool. They're good guys, I promise."

"What do you mean his rank is higher? Do you mean Bruno is actually…"

"The less you know, the better."

"Fine. I'll accept that."

Everyone arrived at Paradise Café safely at 12 noon. Jay and Maria had never felt an earthquake before so they were a little rattled. Dr. King had appetizers and a pitcher of sangria ready for everyone but handed a soda to Maria.

"Hello everyone. This is an unexpected meeting and what a jolt we had this morning. I'm so glad all of you are safe. Was there any damage to your homes?"

"A few glasses broke in our kitchen and I have to check our balcony for cracks," replied Juan.

Everyone else said their homes were fine but Bruno wanted to check Samantha's and Margaret's balcony to be sure.

"I won't be opening my doors until tomorrow evening. I'm giving my staff time to recover. Who's up for some golf?"

The girls finished eating and went to Sand Dollar Jewelers while the men went to play golf.

Friday was a productive day for Maria. Most of the shops were closed so she got a lot of business. Her muscles ached like never before so she spent over an hour in the hot tub when she got home. Everyone is meeting for breakfast at The Ritz Carlton at 7:30 am so Maria can get to her shop before 10. Melanie showed up last wearing a casual printed long sun dress with flat sandals, a white sweater, and Aviator sunglasses that she refused to take off because she wasn't wearing makeup.

"This is the second day in a row I've gotten up at the butt-crack of dawn. First there was an earthquake and now you guys want to eat super early. What gives? I'm on Vegas time. I don't get up before 10."

"It's the same time here doll face," Bruno replied as he poured her some strong coffee.

Melanie and Margaret were going to play tennis later while Jay and Samantha were going Christmas shopping. Juan was going to help Maria for a couple of hours and then rehearse at Paradise Café. Bruno was going to spend time at the hotel making phone calls and do some shopping online. Juan's phone rang. It was Billy.

"Excuse me. I have to take this."

Juan took his phone to the balcony to talk to Billy for five minutes and watch the surfers in the ocean.

"That was Billy. He tried to fly in last night but the airport was closed. He finally got a flight this afternoon. We are playing tonight at Paradise Café. Are we all meeting there tonight for dinner?"

Everyone agreed to meet at 7:30pm.

"I'm taking a disco nap after tennis," said Melanie.

It was a casual evening at Paradise Café with 60 people; most of them wearing jeans and pullover sweaters.

'Billy and the Band' wasn't advertised so the regulars were happy to eat 'Earthquake Nachos' while listening to great music. Maria didn't have to open her shop until 11am so she was able to stay out late and listen to Juan play the piano with the band. As it grew later, the music got softer. People slowly left until it was just the band, the staff, and Maria sitting with Gwen King. Melanie and Margaret lit candles on the balcony at Margaret's beach house and shared a bottle of wine until 3am.

Jay and Samantha got up early Sunday morning. Samantha had to work and Jay had to fly back to NYC. They didn't want to wake anyone and that's why they said 'goodbye' last night. Maria slept until 9am and Juan went to The Ritz to meet Bruno and Billy for golf. Margaret and Melanie slept in and then did some shopping. Melanie was flying back to Las Vegas with Bruno on his private jet at 6:30pm. It was nice to know people in high places. Bruno was a friend for life. Maria was looking forward to closing the shop at 5pm to spend time with Juan. After locking up, Maria took a sigh of relief at her successful weekend and knew her shop will do well during the holidays. She felt Jack's spirit all around her as she drove home to be with the love of her life.

CHAPTER 13

Maria woke up to the beautiful sound of Juan playing his grand piano. It was mid-December and Juan was practicing for his New Year's Eve show in Las Vegas. He will be playing with Billy and the Band and the show is already sold out. Sand Dollar Jewelers has been very busy and Margaret has been helping Maria daily during this holiday season. Jay was in NYC working and wouldn't see Samantha until after Christmas. Samantha was on her way to Vegas to spend time with Melanie and Bruno. Bruno was still attracted to Samantha but didn't tell anyone. He had a thing for flight attendants. Bruno and Juan have been talking a lot on the phone. Juan wants to propose to Maria and would like Bruno's help getting a ring. Juan found out her ring size from Margaret so he can get the ball rolling. Bruno has been sending email pictures to Juan from a jeweler in Las Vegas. One thing Bruno knows is how to buy cars and diamonds. Bruno was sitting on a bar stool in Melanie's kitchen looking at his laptop.

"Do you want to see the ring Juan is buying for Maria?"

"Did he decide to propose? Oh, my God! It's beautiful. She will be so happy. Does she know?"

"I don't think so. He's proposing on Christmas."

The ring was a canary yellow three carat diamond set in white gold with baguettes on both sides.

"So, what time is Sam getting here?"

"Is that why you're hanging around? You want to see her? You still have a thing for her."

"Maybe. I want to be there to pick up the pieces when douche bag breaks her heart again."

"Do you think he learned his lesson?"

"No. It's just a matter of time before he cheats again. I'll try not to hurt him physically," Bruno said sarcastically.

"You're in luck. I just received a text. Her plane just landed."

Melanie called her driver to bring the car around. He brought the black limo with a red ribbon on the driver's side door and front passenger door. They were 14-inch removable magnets. Melanie was working on an AIDS charity this month and it showed her appreciation for the victims and survivors.

"What do you think she'll be hungry for?" asked Bruno.

"You are always thinking about food."

"I also think about women and smoking a nice cigar."

"In that order?"

"No, the women come first."

It was a fifteen-minute ride to the airport. There was just enough time for Melanie to make drinks in the limo bar.

Samantha was waiting on the curb and saw the limo pull up and Bruno got out. Her heart stopped for a moment. He looked more handsome than usual. She got in and they agreed on Italian takeout. They went to the restaurant and Samantha and Melanie waited in the limo and drank while Bruno went inside to get the food.

"What hotel is Juan going to be playing at?"

"The Bellagio," Melanie replied.

"Do you think we have backstage passes?"

"I'm almost positive we do. It's going to be a blast."

"I hope Jay booked a room for that weekend. It's only two weeks away."

"If not, the two of you may stay with me. Margaret's staying with me and there is plenty of room for more."

"Thanks. I'll keep that in mind. I better text Jay to see what's going on. I've been all over the Midwest and I haven't had a chance to get in touch with him."

Bruno came out of the restaurant with two large paper bags. There was enough food to have leftovers and they headed home. Jay got back to Samantha and wanted her to Skype later so they can talk again. The three of them got home and ate and then got in the hot tub. It was a relaxing evening. Bruno was getting calls from The Bellagio Hotel. He had a cousin that was the General Manager of the resort and needed a new grand piano for the Diana Krall concert tomorrow night. It must be tuned and ready to go and it was too late to borrow one from another resort. Bruno got out of the hot tub and excused himself. He knew someone that owned a piano warehouse and off he went.

"He sure left in a hurry, didn't he?" asked Samantha.

"He sure did but it was an emergency and this happens a lot during the holidays. He knows so many people in town and he gets the job done."

"He's not a dangerous man, is he? I mean, sometimes he can be sketchy."

"I know what you mean but he is safe. Some of his friends are shady but I know he hasn't hurt anyone. He knows people in the FBI and they come around the club to keep things in line. They know his family is connected to organized crime but Bruno is not part of that. That's why he left Jersey. It's safer here."

"You'd think it would be the other way around. Vegas was discovered by the Mob and some members are still here and always will be. That lifestyle gets passed down from generation to generation."

"That is true but so does the FBI; except the FBI is a smaller organization and you also have people playing for both sides," said Melanie as she took her last sip of wine.

The ladies relaxed a few minutes more before Samantha went upstairs to Skype Jay and get ready for bed.

Maria came home at 8pm after a 12-hour shift of undecided male shoppers trying to buy jewelry for their wives or mistresses. Juan was on the staircase in a Santa hat stringing Christmas lights on the banister and listening to Christmas carols.

"Wow! This place looks amazing! I especially like the big wreath outside. Are we having a party this year?"

"Yes, but only a small one. Fifteen people at the most. Do you think our friends will agree to come over on the 24th?"

"I can email everyone right now," answered Maria. "It smells good in here. Are you baking something?"

"Meatloaf. Are you hungry?"

"I'm starving. You're so domestic."

"After dinner I will rub your feet."

Maria peeked around the corner and stared at Juan. "Are you serious?"

"Of course. You worked all day."

"So have you. Is Billy coming over tomorrow to go over the new songs?"

"Yes, and then we will go over to Paradise Café to rehearse. The concert is sold out now."

"I'm not surprised. I'm going to have Margaret open the shop tomorrow so I can sleep in. She's doing a great job with sales. I'm keeping her on as a full-time employee after the holidays."

The xeric weather had the birds and squirrels running about in Central Park, New York as Jay finished his run and walked the rest of the way to his Manhattan penthouse. Listening to classical music on his iPod was he enjoyed while running. He ignored all texts until he got home. When he got home he poured Fiji water into a tall glass and drank the refreshing water and caught up on texts and emails. He received the email from Maria and replied but never responded to Samantha's text. For some reason, he wasn't missing her that much and he hasn't bought her a gift yet for Christmas. He read the weather report and there will be snowfall tomorrow. Finally, the first snow of the season.

Las Vegas was getting a lot of rain and the streets were flooded. Three women called off at Bruno's club because some of the roads were closed. Bruno decided to take his Hummer vehicle so he can make it to the club to do his paperwork. All he can think about is Samantha and everything he loved about her. His feelings for her were getting stronger but he had to control them since she was taken. He decided to call Melanie as soon as he arrived at the club.

"Hey Mel."

"Hi. What's going on?"

"I just got to work. It'll be a slow day. The weather is shitty."

"I know. I'm staying in today."

"The reason why I called is, I want to get Sam a Christmas gift but I don't want to step on any toes. Do you think it's appropriate?"

"I knew you were falling for her. She's still with Jay you know. Why don't you come by tonight and we will discuss it."

"Ok. How does 6:30 sound?"

"Perfect. See you then. Bye Bruno."

"Bye."

Melanie immediately got on the phone and called Samantha to see what state she was in.

"Hi Mel. Can I call you when I get to Santa Barbara? I'm getting on the plane now. I'm leaving Honolulu. I was only here for three hours. It wasn't enough time to leave the airport."

"Ok. I'll talk to you soon. Bye."

"Bye."

The flight to California took over five hours and Samantha was glad to be home. She checked her messages and responded to Maria's invitation. So far everyone was going to Maria's home on Christmas Eve.

Everyone made it to Santa Barbara already except Jay. He was still in NYC scrambling for a gift to give Samantha and had no idea what to get her. He walked into Tiffany, looked around and walked right out. Jay didn't feel secure enough in the relationship to give Samantha jewelry. He walked down to Macy's and bought her a silk blouse and called his driver to put his packed luggage in the trunk and take him to the airport. He didn't have time to go home.

Bruno was checked in to The Ritz Carlton and Billy was staying with Maria and Juan. Melanie stayed with Margaret in her brand-new room. Melanie had enough money to buy her own beach house but enjoyed Margaret's company. Bruno called Samantha and invited her to the hotel lounge so she put on a little black dress and out the door she went.

Samantha was looking elegant with her sparkly black dress and shiny black stilettos. The valet attendant opened her car door and the bellmen stopped what they were doing. Their heads turned as she walked by with the aroma of her perfume in the air. She was a vision in the night. She walked past the Christmas decorations on her way to the lounge and spotted Bruno on a bar stool. He was looking more dapper than ever. He turned and stood up to greet Samantha. Bruno was wearing a white silk shirt and gray slacks and smelled nice. His gold chain sparkled against his chest and he kissed Samantha on the cheek and ordered her a drink.

"What are we doing here? I feel guilty but happy at the same time," said Samantha.

"I wanted to spend time with you before Jay gets here. I have a gift for you and I can't give it to you at the party. When does Jay get here?"

Samantha looked surprised.

"You didn't have to get me anything. Jay will be here before midnight."

"Only Melanie knows about this gift."

Bruno handed Samantha a long velvet box. She opened it carefully and saw the most beautiful tennis bracelet she had ever seen. The diamonds sparkled under the light as a tear rolled down Samantha's cheek.

"I can't believe this! It's so beautiful!"

"You deserve it. Let me put it on you."

Samantha gave Bruno a quick kiss on the lips. The bracelet looked perfect with her red finger nails.

"I can't tell anyone about this can I?"

"You can, just not Jay. I know he's your boyfriend but the man is not reliable and he can't give you what you need. If you want me to back off I will but I don't want to. I care for you so much."

"I know you do. I care for you also. I just don't want to get confused."

"No need for confusion. I will leave you alone at the party tomorrow. I know Jay will be there," said Bruno.

The two of them took their drinks and went to the pool to find a quiet bench.

Jay arrived in Chicago to change planes only to find his connecting flight is delayed four hours. He went to the nearest bar for beer and pizza holding his Macy's Christmas bag with the silk blouse inside. The bartender was an attractive blonde woman with a tight polo shirt. Jay immediately texted Samantha but she ignored her phone to be with Bruno.

"Do you want to answer your phone? It keeps vibrating," asked Bruno.

"It's probably Jay."

"All the more reason…"

Back at Juan and Maria's house, they finished dinner and listened to Christmas carols while Billy poured eggnog. Margaret and Melanie watched 'It's a Wonderful Life' at Margaret's beach house and Jay sat at the Chicago airport bar waiting for Samantha to text back. Bruno and Samantha held hands at The Ritz Carlton pool and finished their drinks.

"I should walk you to the valet before I invite you up to my room," said Bruno jokingly.

"Good idea."

Samantha got in the car and rolled down her window and Bruno handed the valet attendant $20 and told him to keep it.

"I'll see you tomorrow at the party," said Samantha.

"I'll be dreaming about you tonight."

Samantha smiled and drove off into the night. The moon was full and yellow and she couldn't help but stare at the bracelet between traffic lights. When she finally arrived home she went straight to her balcony to listen to the ocean waves and stare at the moon and returned the texts from Jay.

CHAPTER 14

Samantha's phone vibrated at 6am. It was a text from Jay. His plane just landed in Santa Barbara and he was not happy with the situation. He waved his madcap arm to get a taxi to take him to Samantha's house. He didn't want to show up in a bad mood so he took a deep breath. Samantha made coffee and she noticed Margaret on her balcony drinking her coffee.

"Hello stranger. What are you doing up so early?" asked Samantha.

"Hi. I couldn't sleep. Mel is still sleeping. I'll probably nap later. Is Jay asleep?"

"No. He's on his way. That's why I'm up."

"You mean he's not here yet?"

"No. He was delayed in Chicago."

"What's that smile? Why are you grinning?"

"I didn't really miss him. His schedule is unpredictable and I didn't count on him being here although I'm glad he's on his way."

"Wait a second. What's going on?"

They both smiled at each other.

"I'll tell you after the party. I have to feel things out first."

"Oh my God. Did you meet someone?"

"I meet a lot of people."

"You know what I mean. Do you want to come over later?"

"Possibly. Jay's cab is here. I better go"

"Good luck."

"Thanks. I'll talk to you later."

Samantha opened the door and waited for Jay while he paid the driver.

"Hi babe! I finally made it."

"I'm glad. It was a long night for you. Are you hungry?"

"No. I just want to lie down for a while."

"Ok."

Jay kissed Samantha quickly on the lips and went to the bedroom. He didn't even hug her. They hadn't seen each other in a month and for him it was just another day. Their relationship was becoming platonic.

It was already 12 noon so Samantha checked on Jay to see if he was still sleeping. She made herself a sandwich and took a walk on the beach with Melanie and Margaret.

"How is Jay doing?" asked Margaret.

"He hasn't said two words to me yet. He's still sleeping."

"Have you talked to Bruno? You know he's at The Ritz, right?" asked Melanie as though she knew every detail.

"Do you know something?"

"I know about that beautiful bling on your wrist," smiled Melanie.

"Oh my God! That's amazing! Who gave that to you?" asked Margaret.

"I'd rather not say."

"You don't have to. I helped him pick it out," said Melanie.

"Why doesn't that surprise me?"

"Wait a second. You and Bruno are an item? I'm confused," said Margaret with a puzzled look.

"He just has a crush. That's all."

"It's more than a crush," replied Melanie.

"Is Bruno trying to sabotage what you and Jay have?" asked Margaret.

"Sam and Jay don't have much. Their relationship is turning to dust. No offense," said Melanie.

"None taken. I like the attention Bruno gives me. He treats me like a lady. Jay treats me like one of the guys and he can be rude and abrasive at times. I keep asking myself if he's going to cheat again. He thinks we've moved past that, but I don't think that I have. It's always in the back of my mind."

A sand dollar washed up on the shore and Melanie picked it up.

"Jack must be listening. I'll give this to Maria tonight," smiled Melanie.

Samantha went back home and found Jay awake and ready to eat everything in the kitchen. He was playing soft music and swaying in the kitchen while eating his bagel.

"How's the jetlag?"

"I seem to be recovering. Come dance with me. It's Christmas Eve and I feel good."

"Okay, but its 3pm. I need to pick up the Cuban pastries from the bakery before they close."

"Alright. What time do we have to leave?"

"Six o'clock."

Samantha left for the bakery and was tempted to text Bruno but she didn't. She stared at her beautiful bracelet and thought Jay would ask about it but never did.

The party at Maria and Juan's home was getting underway. The bartender from Paradise Café was there to bartend and Dr. Gwen King was the last to show up. Bruno and Samantha barely said anything to each other but kept smiling at one another. Jay spent half his time on his cell phone talking to people in New York and making New Year's Eve plans for his restaurant.

Billy played the piano and Juan sang Christmas carols. Juan wanted to propose to Maria before dinner. Very few people knew about this. He called Maria over and everyone stood around the white grand piano. Jay put his arm around Samantha's waist as Juan spoke.

"Maria, when I first met you, I knew you were someone special. You have lived an interesting life and you are the sister of someone dear to our hearts. You are beautiful, smart, and strong and I know Jack is watching over you every day and would love to be here at this party but it's time for me to take care of you now." Juan got down on one knee and opened a velvet box. "Maria, will you please marry me?"

Maria's eyes opened wide. "Oh my God! Juan! Yes! Yes, I'll marry you!" They hugged and Maria cried while everyone clapped. Jay's phone rang and he immediately excused himself and went to the backyard. Melanie handed the sand dollar to Maria. She turned it over and it had the date written with a Sharpie.

"Jack *is* here at this party. Now you can't forget the day you got engaged."

"This is beautiful. Thank you. I'll keep it at the jewelry store."

"I found it this morning. That's how I knew something special was going to happen today."

"I love it."

Billy played the piano some more before dinner. The ladies put platters of food in the kitchen so everyone could serve themselves buffet style. Bruno walked over to Samantha.

"Maybe you should tell your boyfriend that dinner is ready. He's still in the backyard."

"I know. I'll get him or, maybe not," Samantha said jokingly.

Jay saw Samantha coming and ended the call.

"Dinner is ready."

"Ok. Sorry, I was making plans with my managers for New Year's Eve."

"I'm glad you're getting it covered because we'll be in Vegas for Juan's concert."

"Oh, I can't go to Vegas."

"What?! Why not? What do you mean?"

"New Year's Eve is the busiest night of the year. My restaurant is in Time Square. I have to be there."

"I thought you had managers to cover that."

"I do but what if they need me? I haven't missed a year yet. If something goes wrong, I'm screwed."

"You can't control everything. I'm sure your staff will know what to do in an emergency."

"We'll talk about this later. Let's eat."

Jay walked away and left Samantha standing next to the fountain. She turned around and saw a shooting star fly across the sky above the mission. Her eyes began to tear but she wasn't about to let Jay's insouciance get the best of her. She saw Bruno looking her way and decided to go inside. Jay served himself and sat down at the bar and ordered himself a cocktail not caring what Samantha was doing. Bruno followed Samantha after she served herself and he whispered in her ear.

"Is everything okay?"

"Jay is not going to Vegas. He'd rather work."

Bruno smiled. "Gee, what a shame."

"Stop that," smiled Samantha.

"You deserve better. You'll still have fun. I'll show you my club and you could meet some of the ladies. They are all classy and educated. I only hire beautiful students. There is nothing sleazy about it."

"I know. Mel told me all about it. It sounds like a plan."

"You should go sit next to Jay and pretend to have a good time. We'll talk later."

Jay finally stopped giving Samantha the silent treatment and danced with her. A slow song came on and Juan cut in. "Excuse me sir, may I dance with your lady?"

"Of course."

"So, how are things?" asked Juan.

"Ok. Congratulations by the way."

"Thank you. Are you changing the subject?"

"Maybe. Jay is not going to make it to the concert in Vegas. He has other plans."

"That's alright. Maybe next time. Will there be a next time? You know, sometimes things happen for a reason. He might not be the right man for you."

"I'm starting to think that."

A few minutes later all of the ladies went to the kitchen to put the food away and all of the men went to the bar to talk sports. The party was coming to a close and people started to leave. Dr. King was the last to leave and she was so happy about the engagement and couldn't wait to hear Juan and Billy play in Vegas. Billy kissed Dr. King on the cheek and went upstairs to bed and Gwen King went home. The party was a true success. Who ever thought a Christmas/House-warming/Engagement party would be so beautiful?

Samantha woke up early to find a Christmas package on her kitchen table. She read the card and it was from Jay. She wasn't sure at first because the girls next door had a key and it was Christmas morning but she didn't think they would rise this early. Jay was still sleeping. He had a lot to drink last night so Samantha let him sleep. He never even wanted to make love or ask for a 'rain check'. Samantha whispered in his ear. "May I open my present now?"

Jay slowly opened his eyes. "Yeah. Bring it here. I want to see you open it."

Samantha went to the kitchen to get the gift and also brought his from under the tree. They both opened their gifts and he was very happy that she bought him a new iPad and she thought her cheap sweater was nice. 'It's the thought that counts', she thought to herself.

She has many sweaters and will probably never wear it. She let him go back to sleep and she went next door to exchange gifts with Melanie and Margaret and then they took a walk on the beach to meet Bruno half way. It was only one mile to The Ritz Carlton and they wanted to burn off the sweets they had last night. Samantha and Bruno were looking forward to seeing each other and the girls were glad Jay stayed behind. Melanie and Margaret liked Bruno much better and didn't care much for Jay.

They finally reached Bruno and he hugged all three of the ladies. Samantha spoke to Bruno. "I didn't get you a gift but the next time I'm in Vegas, I will make you dinner."

"Just having you in my life is a gift," replied Bruno. Samantha looked at him in shock. It was the sweetest thing a man could say.

They talked for thirty minutes and the ladies went back home. Jay was awake on the balcony playing with his new iPad and drinking coffee.

"Are we going to lay in bed today and watch '*It's a Wonderful Life*? asked Samantha.

"No. Actually, my flight is in three hours so I need to take a shower and get going. Did I forget to mention it?" Samantha looked puzzled.

"Yes, you did forget to mention it. You just got here yesterday."

"Sorry babe. I have a lot of work to do."

"Go get in the shower. I'll drop you off at the airport."

Samantha texted Bruno so they can meet later.

Samantha drove Jay to the airport in silence and it didn't even phase him since he was on the phone most of the ride there. She dropped him off at the curb and he kissed her on the cheek. This was the most affection she received from him the whole 24-hour trip. Off he went and he didn't look back to wave at her. She thought he was a complete jackass as she drove off. She pulled into a Denny's parking lot so she could cry for a few minutes. Jay's spiteful attitude ruined her Christmas and she knew she had to make a decision whether to keep him as a boyfriend or part ways. Samantha received a text from Bruno and she immediately headed to The Ritz to have a drink at the lounge.

Bruno had a Cosmopolitan waiting for Samantha and he had his usual scotch on the rocks. They hugged when she arrived and of course her eyes were red from crying.

"Do you want to tell me what happened?"

"I just dropped Jay off at the airport. He didn't even stay the whole day and he was in a hurry to leave. I don't know why he came in the first place. He should have stayed in NY. The trip was a waste."

"Do you want my opinion?"

"Sure, why not."

"He wanted to see you one last time but was too afraid to break up with you. I think he wants you to make the first move so he will be off the hook. It's not easy to break up with someone during the holidays."

"I'm going to have to let him go. He's not worth it."

"No, he's not. Did he at least get you a gift?"

"Yes, a shitty sweater."

They both smiled and laughed.

"I would love to take you upstairs and have you spend the night but that wouldn't be the answer," said Bruno.

"I know."

"Tomorrow is another day," he said as they held hands.

CHAPTER 15

Christmas had come and gone quickly and Maria and Margaret worked side by side expecting jewelry returns. There weren't any so far. All of the customers seemed happy with their purchases.

"You look happy these days; more than usual. You must be enjoying your engagement," said Margaret.

"I sure am. I never thought he would propose this soon. It's been less than a year since Jack died and every time I dream about him, he is smiling."

"He must approve."

The ladies were flying together to Las Vegas. Juan was already there with Billy, and Samantha was flying in from Salt Lake City. Samantha didn't have to work the East Coast until next week.

Melanie picked up Samantha at the airport in her usual limo fashion and Bruno would catch up with them for dinner. Margaret had her own suite at The Bellagio and was ready to start dating again. It was almost a new year and she needed a man in her life. She spent many years as a single lady. Melanie didn't mind being single for now. She had her charities to keep her busy. Samantha called Jay but he didn't answer the phone. He wanted to end things on his terms. Samantha emailed him and said she would be in NYC in two weeks to talk.

The concert was sold out and Maria and Margaret went to the auditorium to watch the band practice. There was a nice gentleman in his mid-50's with silver hair watching the performance. Apparently, he was a friend of Billy's and had invested a lot of time and money into his band. He was now a real estate mogul in Las Vegas and kept staring at Margaret. The two of them introduced themselves and went out for drinks soon after. His name was Gary and he happened to be single.

Melanie woke up to the chirping birds on her balcony. She opened her French doors and noticed a nest on the light fixture. She didn't want to disturb it but wanted to see inside so she went to get a stool and a mirror and angled it just right to see four small eggs that belonged to the Blue Jay that came by every morning. She thought it was the sweetest thing so she woke up Samantha so she could see them.

"Are you really getting me up to see some crazy bird?"

"She is the sweetest bird and she has a nest with four eggs."

"Speaking of eggs, are you making breakfast?"

Samantha got up on the stool and used the mirror to see inside the nest.

"Oh, my… That is so cute! Where is mother bird now?"

"She is in that tree waiting for us to leave. Let's go inside and see what she does."

Mother Blue Jay flew back to her nest and chirped some more. Bruno called the girls to see if they wanted dinner later at his favorite Italian restaurant. Everyone else had plans at Bellagio before the concert and Juan had to rest his voice so he wasn't talking. Dinner would be at Mario's near Bruno's house and then straight to the concert after that.

"I just received a text from Margaret. She met a sexy man last night at the rehearsal. His name is Gary, mid-50's, tall, brown skin, silver wavy hair, blue eyes, and nice teeth," said Samantha.

"What's his last name? I might know him."

"I'll find out. I believe his name is Gary Jackson."

"I know him. He has money. He comes to a lot of charity events. He's super handsome."

"I think everyone has a date tonight except you. Are you going to settle down again someday?"

"Probably not. When I was dancing I slept with a lot of men and then I met the man of my dreams, got married, and now I'm a widow. Do I really want to do that again? I'm content right now and I have a lot of male friends but who's to say I won't meet someone? You just never know."

The ladies ate breakfast and went through Melanie's glamorous closet to find something to wear for the black-tie concert. Melanie and Samantha were the same height and body type but Melanie had larger breasts due to enhancement. Samantha was always wearing Melanie's clothes and Melanie had a black American Express Card with no limit so she could buy what she likes and many of her clothes went to charity. Samantha decided on a royal blue sequins gown by Vera Wang.

Melanie opened the safe built into the floor of her closet to get the Cartier jewels her husband left her.

"Here. This one matches that gown," said Melanie.

"Are you fucking serious? That's a million-dollar necklace! I'm not wearing it."

"1.3 million. And yes, you are wearing it. I want you to look stunning for Bruno."

"I can't believe it. What if something happens to it?"

"It's insured so who cares."

"I think you had too many Mimosas and you are not thinking clearly."

Melanie settled on a red gown by Dolce and Gabbana.

"I hate to bring this up but have you heard from Jay?"

"No, I haven't. I don't think I love him anymore. I haven't thought about him all day. I'll be in New York City on the 10th and quell what's left of the relationship. He doesn't even want to communicate with me. He's married to his job."

"You don't need someone like that. He's unreliable."

Melanie's driver picked up the ladies at 5pm to take them to Mario's restaurant to meet Bruno. The ladies waited to have a drink until they got to the restaurant. Melanie knew there would be a $300 bottle of Cabernet sitting on the table.

When the limo arrived, the valet attendant opened the car door and out came Melanie first and then Samantha. Bruno was on the curb waiting for them in his gray Armani tux and for the first time he was nervous. He wanted to impress Samantha but there was no need. She was already impressed and happier than she's been in ages. The

Maître D' wore a black tuxedo and white gloves and showed the three of them to their corner table by the fireplace.

"You ladies look stunning as usual."

"Thank you, Bruno. This place is lovely," said Samantha as she touched her necklace to make sure it was still there.

"I wonder if Mario Jr. is here tonight. His father, Mario Sr., opened this place in 1960 and it still has that swank feel of that time," said Melanie.

A sommelier came by and poured sparkling water and opened the bottle of wine. A server brought delicious garlic bread to enjoy. There were at least four people waiting on each table with a different job to do. The restaurant was half full. Bruno made a toast to the New Year and the server took their picture. They had great conversation and ate their Caesar salads. Bruno put his hand on Samantha's lap and kissed her cheek. They acted like a loving couple. Samantha thought it would be rude to pull out her cell phone to check her text messages so she waited until they were done with the salads so she can excuse herself to the restroom.

"Excuse me. I must use the ladies' room."

"Of course," said Bruno as he stood up and put her napkin on the back of her chair. She couldn't believe he was such a gentleman. No one had ever treated her with such respect.

"I don't want to ask Sam if she's heard from Jay. Do you know if she has?" asked Bruno.

"Not yet. I'm sure that's why she went to the bathroom; to see if he left a message. You have nothing to worry about. She's almost done with him. He's a tool and she knows it. She's going to break it off."

"I know, but the last time she went to New York City she ended up in bed with him."

"That won't happen this time. She won't make that same mistake twice. I'm going to suggest I go with her for emotional support."

"That would be terrific."

Samantha freshened up and checked her phone. There were no messages and she felt relieved. Maybe Jay will text at midnight but she didn't want to think about him until then. She walked back to the table and Bruno stood up again and helped her with her chair and he put the napkin back on her lap. Dinner came and all three of them had Eggplant Parmesan. It was delicious. They enjoyed their dinner and finished the bottle of wine and had Spumoni for dessert.

"Bruno, you should leave your car here and we can take the limo to The Bellagio," suggested Melanie.

"That is the plan and after, we can walk around until midnight. We can watch the water fountain show."

"I will have to find a plus-one if you want me to tag along. I'll check my phone and see who is on reserve."

"That figures," laughed Bruno.

Bruno paid the bill with his Black AMEX and left a 30% tip. As they got up to go outside Melanie whispered in Samantha's ear.

"So, did Jay send you a text?"

"No, nothing."

"That's a good thing."

"Tell me about it."

They got in the limo and off they went into the heavy traffic.

"I think the whole world is here in Vegas. Look at all of the cops," said Bruno. There was a road block every two miles or so it seemed. Melanie received a text from Billy and he wanted her to spend time with the band after the concert. Many celebrities would be there so she accepted.

They arrived backstage at 7:30 and they saw Maria and she looked amazing in a purple Oscar de la Renta gown with a white gold necklace she borrowed from her own store.

"Maria!" said Melanie.

"Oh, my God! Hi you guys! Isn't this exciting? I am so nervous." Maria squeezed both Melanie's and Samantha's hand.

"This is a piece of cake for Juan. He's done this a million times honey," said Melanie. Bruno kissed Maria on the cheek. "You look beautiful as always."

"Thank you."

"Is Juan nervous?" asked Samantha.

"I don't think so. Margaret's in the restroom. She'll be right out."

Someone in a tuxedo handed them glasses of champagne and showed them to their seats. Margaret came out of the restroom wearing a floral dress and Gary followed behind.

"Samantha, this is Gary. Bruno, have you met Gary?"

"Yes, a few years ago. Hello. Nice to see you again."

Gary kissed the back of Melanie's and Samantha's hand.

"I've heard great things about you Gary," said Samantha.

Everyone took their seats and the lights dimmed and the crowd roared and clapped. The lights showed brightly on stage and a grand piano rolled out on the platform with Juan playing a jazz number. The audience stood up and clapped and Juan began to sing. Twenty minutes later Billy and The Band came out with their soft rock style. Their performances were brilliant and the concert lasted two hours. The friends gathered around while Juan signed and gave away CD's for another 45 minutes and then they went to his suite for champagne and strawberries. The view was incredible from the 10th floor and it overlooked the famous fountain.

"We should go down there and see the midnight water show. It's a sight to see," suggested Bruno.

"Alright. We'll have to get there a little early. People will start lining up on the strip for that," replied Samantha.

"I'm enjoying this evening. I haven't been this happy in years. Good friends, good music, and good food. It doesn't get better than this," said Bruno as he kissed Samantha on the cheek. Margaret and Gary agreed to go to the strip with Bruno and Samantha and then take Bruno to the restaurant to pick up his car. The four of them hugged everyone 'goodbye' and went down to the crowded strip.

The four of them found a spot close to the rail of the fountain; in the center and there were many people. They couldn't move if they wanted to. The show started at 11:40 and will end at midnight with fireworks. The show was incredible as Bruno held Samantha to keep her warm. Margaret took a video with her cell phone and heard the countdown to midnight and the water continued to dance and sway. The crowd roared at midnight.

After taking pictures Samantha looked at her phone to see if Jay called or texted and there wasn't anything. It was 3am in NY so Jay was probably on his way home to have his final drink and probably with a woman. Samantha didn't care and actually felt relieved. It will make the breakup easier.

"Did he call?" asked Bruno.

"Did who call?"

"Jay. Did he call? It's none of my business. I'm sorry."

"No, he didn't call. I'll be in NY in two weeks to break it off."

"The choice is yours. I don't want to persuade you either way."

"I know. You've been a gem. Thank you."

They hugged and the four of them walked to the valet to get Gary's car.

"Gary, are you ok to drive?" asked Margaret.

"I had half a glass of champagne. I knew I'd be driving. I'm good."

"Ok."

Bruno held Samantha's hand as they walked.

"Do you want to see where I work? Would you like to go to my club and meet some of the girls? No pressure," asked Bruno.

"Really? That would be so amazing! I'd love to. Are you able to drive?"

"Yes. I haven't drunk since dinner and that was six hours ago; that's why I poured my champagne into your glass at the concert.

Bruno and Samantha arrived at his club and the bouncer opened the door for them. Samantha couldn't believe how glamorous the place was. It was very classy. The lights were dim but the spotlights were on the two runways. The women dancing were very beautiful. Bruno only picked the best and did background checks on all of them and random drug testing. All of his dancers were students and this is where Melanie used to dance. They walked into the dressing room and two ladies were putting on makeup and wearing silk robes. They looked like showgirls and they said 'hello' to Bruno as he introduced Samantha. She noticed a beautiful mural on the far side of the room that was painted with seashells and fish and a nice poem was written in the middle. It was signed by the author. It read:

PURPOSE

A new chapter begins
Expect the unexpected
Lost in the cold;

A different life unfolds

Charming hands reach out
Confusion shuts the door
What is this about?
He walks tall and proud

Small gestures and a smile
Can we be seen?
It only takes a while
He is my reason and my purpose

--- Candace Smith

"That is such a beautiful and spiritual poem. I wish I had that talent. Does Candace work here?"

"Not any more. She's in a better place. She died of breast cancer in July of 2009. She came in and painted that after her last treatment of chemo. She was smiling the whole time like she didn't care that she was sick. Notice the sand dollar at the bottom."

"Oh my… I love this." Samantha smiled with a tear in her eye.

"Let's go to the bar and have a Ginger ale. I'll introduce you to the bartender."

While sitting at the bar Samantha received a text. Her heart stopped for a moment thinking it was Jay. The text was from Melanie. Everyone decided to do a little gambling in the high rollers room at Bellagio and wanted to know if Samantha and Bruno were interested. There were at least four body guards for Juan and Billy so getting through the crowd won't be easy. Samantha decided to get back to her in 15 minutes.

"This is such a nice place, Bruno. You should be proud of it."

"I am proud of it. Thank you. Sometimes I have relatives come in. You know, the ones in organized crime. I make sure they don't stay long. I don't want them to tarnish the place."

"So, do you think we should go back to Bellagio to gamble?"

"According to this text, Gary is on a winning streak so we should go there."

They went out to the parking lot and got in the car and Bruno kissed Samantha.

"You are the most stunning woman in Las Vegas. It's not the gown or the fancy jewels. You have a natural beauty about you. If you were wearing jeans and a t-shirt and no makeup, you would look just as stunning."

"Thank you. You are not so bad yourself. You make me feel special."

There was a lot of traffic at 2am. Las Vegas never sleeps and it took Bruno and Samantha an hour to get to the casino and it was only three miles from Bruno's club. He found a parking spot and they went inside.

"I wanted to ask you something back at the club," said Samantha.

"Sure, what is it? Let's sit down on this bench right here. There's no hurry."

"You know how you said your relatives come visit the club sometimes?"

"Yes?"

"Does that make you nervous? Do you feel like you owe them anything?"

"Not really. We have an understanding. They only do drastic things as a last resort. They look out for me because they know I'm spiritual and not religious. I don't go to church but I was raised Catholic. Most Italians are Catholic. I don't believe in organized religion."

"But you believe in organized crime? I'm sorry. Was that out of line?"

"Not at all. You have a lot of questions and you're getting to know me still. I have all of the answers. For example, I had a lady working in my club a couple of years ago. She had an abusive ex-boyfriend that was stalking her even though she had a restraining order against him. He was persistent and wouldn't leave her alone. This guy was bad news. She even had a police officer posted outside her home so she would feel safe but the creep still found his way in her home. The cops could only do so much. He would get arrested and a few days later he was out of jail again. I called my cousin and told him what was going on and he took care of it. The man was never seen again and his identity had been erased like he never existed. The lady is safe and now has a loving husband and a baby on the way. She thanks me every Christmas with a card and a nice bottle of wine."

"And what happened to the ex-boyfriend?"

"I don't know. I don't ask questions. I'm not sure I want to know. They would just tell me to forget about it if I asked questions in the past."

"So, in a way they are like guardian angels," said Samantha.

"Something like that."

Bruno kissed the back of her hand and they went off to the casino.

They arrived at the High Roller Craps table and Gary was doing very well. He only had a few chips; $1,000 each chip. Bruno had a $5,000 chip in his pocket that he was saving for a special occasion. Juan knew he had the chip and wanted him to use it. Bruno had to think about it. He didn't want to show off. Gary was almost as wealthy as Bruno and didn't mind a challenge.

"It's not about the money, it's how you play the game, Bruno. Let's do this," said Gary. Bruno put the chip on the table, Samantha picked the number and Margaret rolled the dice. The ladies just realized how much the chip was worth and turned their heads away from the table. The men cheered and the women squealed. Bruno just doubled his money and walked away with ten grand. He doesn't gamble very often. Bruno thinks life is enough of a gamble. The choices he makes on a daily basis are a gamble. Bruno and Samantha stayed for 30 more minutes before cashing in and then went to Melanie's house so Samantha could get some rest and Melanie followed shortly after. They arrived at 3:45am and Samantha took off her shoes, put on Frank Sinatra, and turned on the fireplace with the touch of a button. She went upstairs to put on some sweats but didn't know where to put the jewels since she didn't know the combination to the safe. She saw the velvet case and gently put the necklace in its case and closed it and then reopened it to take one last look and sighed. She closed it slowly as if she would never see it again; which was ridiculous because Melanie would let her borrow it anytime. She didn't think wearing something worth millions was a good idea but if Bruno were to be in her life, she would have to get used to wearing nice jewels. She stared at the bracelet which she hasn't taken off yet. It meant the world to her that Bruno gave it to her and they weren't technically dating yet. She went downstairs and Bruno was making chamomile tea.

"I would like to rub your beautiful feet for 20 minutes before I go. I wish I could take you home with me but something will happen," he said with a smile.

"You're probably right. I need to end the unstable relationship I'm in."

"Melanie wants to go with you to NYC or meet you there."

"I know, she mentioned it. It sounds good to me. That feels good. You have strong hands." Bruno continued to massage her feet.

Melanie walked through the front door with a smile on her face.

"Happy New Year Everyone!"

"Someone had a good night," said Bruno.

"You're not the only one who won money, honey. I won $500. I know it's not much but it will buy groceries for a week."

"Neither of you need money and yet you both won," said Samantha as she sipped her tea.

"I'm going to leave you two girls in a few minutes. May I take you to lunch tomorrow, Sam?"

"Yes, but we need to be close to the airport. My flight is at 2pm and I'm working the flight."

Melanie went upstairs to put on her pajamas and Bruno kissed Samantha passionately.

"I'll be dreaming about you tonight," said Bruno.

"I'll be dreaming about you also."

"Bye Mel. I'm leaving."

"Oh, bye. I'll call you tomorrow night."

Bruno left and the ladies stayed up another thirty minutes to talk.

"Did the two of you have a good time tonight?"

"We did. It was the happiest night of my life. We went to his club for a while and I met a couple of the dancers and we talked about his family."

"Bruno is a good man regardless of his family. He's honest and won't hurt anyone. He has a zero-tolerance policy in his club. All of the girls are clean; even the cops hang out there to make sure. It's legitimate. He's in love with you, you know."

"Yes, I know. I have to take care of my situation with Jay."

"Speaking of Jay, would it be alright if I meet you in NYC in case you need moral support?"

"Of course. I can use the support. I'll be staying at The Marriot hotel. I arrive there on the 14th."

"Did Jay text you tonight?"

"Not a word."

"That figures. That's a blessing. You don't need him."

Meanwhile, back in NYC, the time was now 6:45am and Jay rolled over in his bed to find a blonde woman whom he met in Times Square the night before. He couldn't believe what he had done and only felt remorse for a few minutes. The woman woke up and said, "I should get going. My boyfriend is probably looking for me. I'll see you around sometime."

"Yeah, take care."

Bruno picked up Samantha and she was wearing her flight attendant uniform.

"I love a woman in uniform. It's very classy."

"Thanks. Did you get enough sleep?"

"Yes, I did. I went right to bed as soon as I got home. I would like you to stay with me the next time you are in town. Does that sound ok?"

"Yes, it does. I would like that."

"There is a Southern restaurant near the airport. They serve pot pies, Rueben sandwiches, etc.... How does that sound?"

"I love Rueben sandwiches!"

Melanie came down stairs.

"Hey, you two. Are you leaving already?"

"Yes. I have to run. Thank you for everything and I'll see you in NYC."

"That's the plan."

Bruno and Samantha had an hour before she had to be at the airport so they stopped and had lunch.

"Do you own a gun?" asked Samantha.

"Why? Do you need one?"

"I'm just curious because you own a club and might need protection."

"I have two guns. One at home and one at the club in the safe. I keep them loaded. I don't like guns but I have to have them for protection. The next time you come to Vegas, I will take you to the firing range so you can learn to shoot."

"That sounds like a plan."

Bruno took Samantha to the airport and dropped her off at the curb.

"I'll be in touch," said Samantha as she threw her blazer over her shoulder.

"Please keep me posted and let me know when you'll be back."

"Ok."

They smiled at one another and Samantha walked away to catch her flight.

CHAPTER 16

Samantha walked in to Sand Dollar Jewelers to surprise Maria with a latte.

"Oh, Samantha! I'm glad you're back. Wasn't Vegas a blast?"

Samantha handed the drink to Maria. "Thank you. I haven't had the chance to talk to you. How is everything?" asked Maria.

"All is well. I go to NYC next week to talk with Jay. Hopefully he's available. I haven't heard from him since Christmas."

"Are you serious? That was almost two weeks ago."

"I know but I need to break things off so I can get on with my life."

"I'm getting ready to have lunch as soon as Margaret gets here. Would you like to join me at Paradise Café?"

"I'd love to."

When the ladies arrived at the restaurant, the place looked bare. Dr. King and the staff just finished taking down the Christmas decorations and there were sheets covering the stage and grand piano. The bartender had all of the liquor on the bar and off the shelves for dusting and there were cardboard boxes piled high in the corner.

"Hi ladies. You just missed the lunch rush. Come on in," said Gwen King with her hair in a bun.

The staff started to put green table cloths with lupine center pieces on each table for an award ceremony later in the evening. The ladies ordered a Cobb Salad to split and two iced teas.

"Juan was sensational in Las Vegas. Everyone had a great time," said Samantha.

"He was amazing and I'm so glad *Billy and the Band* was able to play with him."

"Have you set a date for you wedding?"

"No. We are thinking about late Spring. I'm already looking at dresses," said Maria as she sprinkled sugar in her iced tea.

"I'm so happy for you and Juan. How are Margaret and Gary? I've only seen her in passing. We live next door to each other but we keep missing one another. I will call her tonight."

"She and Gary are taking it slow. They are good for each other. He will become humbler and she will become more glamorous. I noticed she is fixing herself up every day and has more confidence."

"She hasn't been in a serious relationship since her husband passed; only a few dates here and there," said Samantha as she sprinkled pepper on her salad.

"When are you going to NYC?"

"Next week. I still haven't heard from Jay. I might call him tonight just to make sure he's ok and to let him know I am coming. I'm still breaking up with him and I hope we can be civil. Melanie is meeting me in New York for emotional support that way I keep my head on straight this time."

The ladies finished their lunch and they were the only table left in the restaurant. Two men came in carrying a giant empty aquarium. Dr. King decided to add a special touch to the place by adding a nice salt-water tank and expensive fish. One of the men decorated the tank with extra fine sand and put a sand dollar in each corner and this made Maria think of Jack and she smiled.

It was nice for Samantha to be on a flight to NYC, sitting in First Class, and being treated well without actually working the flight. She stared out the window and saw the Statue of Liberty as her flight attendant collected her champagne glass and the plane descended for landing. Melanie was on a later flight from Las Vegas just 30 minutes behind her. Samantha's plane landed safely and she proceeded to Baggage Claim wearing her gray pant suit and white blouse. She looked like a business woman getting ready to get the job done. She brought extra luggage to do some therapeutic shopping with Melanie. She finally received a text from her soon-to-be-ex to meet her for breakfast in the morning at the hotel restaurant and she smiled a grin of relief. She answered the text and then received a short text from Bruno. 'XOXO'. He was at a loss for words and didn't want to pressure her. She grabbed both suitcases from the carousel and sat down again. Melanie's plane had already landed and she was on her way. Samantha noticed the beautiful art work on the walls. It was a traveling exhibit of oil-on-canvas paintings of different animals. She especially liked the Golden Retriever with a watercolor background. The artist was Stella Jacob and she Googled the name to find more info.

"Hey dog lover. So good to see you," said Melanie with a smile.

"Hi! Are we going to tear up this town or what?"

"The hotel is over 10 miles away. Should we get a limo?"

"Sounds good," answered Samantha.

The ladies went outside and there were three limos to choose from. They chose the silver one and off they went to the Marriott in Times Square. The traffic was horrendous so it took longer than they thought but it gave them a chance to catch up and drink extra alcohol from the limo bar.

"I know the GM of this hotel and we have a nice suite," said Melanie.

"Of course, you know him…from where?"

"He was a client when I was dancing and he is a friend of Bruno."

They arrived at the hotel and the General Manager was waiting for them to take them to their suite without the hassle of checking in. They arrived at the 15th floor and went in to the suite and everything was dusty rose and white. This room was suited for a woman and saved for female celebrities. The GM opened the drapes and there was a perfect view of the Chrysler Building and the city was all lit up ready to swallow them whole. The GM left and the ladies relaxed and enjoyed the champagne that was chilling on ice.

"It's 7pm. Should we stay in or go out?" asked Samantha with a champagne flute in her hand.

"Go out of course. We can eat and go to a museum. My treat."

The ladies took showers and wore minimal makeup and put on casual clothes.

"Do you want to go to the best pizza place in town?" asked Melanie.

Samantha stared out the window without blinking. "What are you looking at?"

"See that building with the blue lights?"

"Yes. What about it?"

"That's Jay's building. That's where he lives."

"Are you reminiscing? It's ok, you know. Just remember, you have a better man waiting for you in Vegas. Jay was just a stepping stone in the walk of life. We all have men like that in our past."

"You're right. I don't hate him; I just can't be friends with him."

"You don't need to be his friend. That's what women are for."

The ladies walked to the pizza place in their snow boots and jackets. The air was crisp and dry and many people were out-and-about in Times Square. They found a cozy table in the back of the restaurant. The pizza slices were huge and they only needed one each with a glass of wine. It was 9pm and the place was packed. Samantha agreed this was the best pizza she's ever eaten.

"How far is the museum from here? I'm so glad they are open until 11:00."

"It's one block. The fresh air is good for our lungs."

"it actually does feel good. I almost wish Maria and Margaret were here."

"I know but they just took that trip to Vegas two weeks ago. They might not be traveling for a while."

The ladies finished their wine and walked slowly to the museum so they wouldn't slip on the icy sidewalk. There wasn't a dress code but many people were nicely dressed. The man at the door was asking for optional donations. There wasn't a cover charge. Melanie handed him a 100-dollar bill and they went in.

"The Broadway show across the street just let out; that's why all of these people are dressed up."

The paintings were stunning and the energy was pleasant. "What are you going to say to Jay when you talk to him tomorrow? Are you going to let him do most of the talking?"

"He can say what he wants. My mind is made up. We are not compatible anymore."

Samantha and Melanie walked around for an hour and then left the museum to walk back to the hotel. When they arrived, they saw the hotel manager on their way to the elevator.

"You ladies look cold. I'm going to send up some hot chocolate and dessert on the house."

"Thank you so much. That would be lovely."

The ladies put on their silk pajamas and finished the champagne they left and waited for room service.

"Should we watch a 'chick flick' or an action movie?"

"This is New York and it's a semi-romantic weekend so, 'chick flick'."

"Old or new?"

"Old and classic but not too old. Maybe something from the 1980's."

Samantha chose *When Harry Met Sally* and then there was a knock at the door. Room service brought hot chocolate and cheesecake and Melanie tipped him $50.

"How much did you tip him?"

"None of your business. The dessert is free."

"Oh my God. What am I going to do with you?"

"You deserve a nice weekend."

"Thank you for being with me. I need all the support I can get. I know my life will be better without Jay but it still hurts a little. I received a text from Maria and Margaret wishing me the best."

"Of course. They are always thinking of you."

They got up on the bed and rearranged the pillows to get comfortable and drank their hot chocolate and ate the cheesecake. They laughed at the movie on the screen and had a perfect girl's night.

Samantha woke up to her cell phone alarm at 7:30am. She knew Melanie would sleep in and then go to the pool. She looked in the closet for some break-up clothes. She whispered to herself, "What do you wear when you break up with someone?" She looked in the tall mirror and pressed a sweater against her chest while still on the hanger. "Maybe business casual since the weather is cold and the ugly sweater that Jay bought me will be put to good use." Samantha made coffee in the coffee maker and started the shower. While taking a shower, she let the steam take over the whole bathroom and she thought about Jay and how they would take showers together.

Samantha sat in the chair with her white terry cloth robe and a towel wrapped around her head and watched Melanie sleep while she sipped her coffee.

Samantha brushed her teeth and spread her makeup on the counter to see which eyeshadow to wear. She settled for earth tones since it was a breakfast meeting. She put her hair up in a French twist, put gold hoop earrings on and dangled the bracelet on her wrist that she hasn't taken off since Bruno gave it to her. She received a text from Jay. He was downstairs waiting. Her heart stopped for a moment while she finished putting on Melanie's Chanel lipstick. Samantha had never bought anything Chanel because Melanie had loads of it including Christian Dior. She left the suite with her handbag and proceeded to the elevator which opened right away. She hoped it would take longer since she was nervous. She wanted to buy more time. The elevator opened to the lobby and Jay was standing by a tall plant dressed very nicely in gray slacks and a white pull-over sweater. He smelled good, as usual.

"Hello, the sweater fits. It looks nice on you. How have you been?" asked Jay as he kissed her cheek.

"I've been well. You look nice."

"Thank you, you as well. Are you hungry?"

"Yes I am. Is there a wait at the restaurant?"

"I don't believe so."

They proceeded to get a table and the hostess gave them a quiet table by the garden.

"Two coffees please," said Jay

"I'll let your server know."

"I'm a little nervous. I've never had a formal break-up before. Usually, I send an email or make a phone call," said Jay with a smug look on his face.

"That's big of you."

"I guess I deserve that. Let's read the menu first so we can order."

Jay noticed her shiny bracelet. "Is that bracelet new? I've never seen it."

"I got it for Christmas. I was wearing it at the Christmas party. I'm surprised you didn't notice."

"I must have been distracted."

"So, how was your New Years?" asked Samantha. Jay's heart skipped a beat and a rush of guilt flooded his veins as he thought about the strange woman, he had in his bed that morning.

"It was alright. I worked, as usual. Did you enjoy Juan and Billy's concert? It got good reviews."

"It was lovely. I had a great time."

"I know I haven't been a good boyfriend to you." The server came and took their order before he could finish what he was saying.

"You were saying…?" Samantha smiled.

"We are not good together. I'm too promiscuous and a workaholic and a lot of other things. You deserve to be with someone nice and loyal."

"No argument there. I still want to be friends. You're not a bad person; just not the type to settle down right now."

"I wish I was ready to settle down. I'm old enough and I have everything I can ask for."

"Someday you will meet the right woman that will change everything for you and then you'll want to settle down and get married and have a couple of kids, etc."

"I know. I thought you were her but I ruined everything and my unfaithfulness is something no woman should put up with."

"At least you admit what the problem is. You can improve it that area. We all have faults."

Jay had tears in his eyes as they finished their breakfast and he paid the bill while holding Samantha's hand on the table. He walked her to the elevator; she stepped in and they stared at one another as the doors closed. She did not shed a tear and she felt relieved and free. She arrived at the suite and went inside. Samantha knew Melanie was at the gym so she opened the drapes and stared out the window for a minute while drinking her sparkling water. Melanie walked in.

"You're back. How did everything go?"

"Pretty well actually. I feel relieved."

"Is that what you wore? Not bad. I would've worn something with cleavage and maybe stilettos. Let him know what he'll be missing."

They both laughed. "Are you ready to shop or what? I'll take a quick shower and then we'll head to Barney's."

"That's expensive."

"Macy's and Sears are across the street. I just want you to experience Barney's since you've never been there. I'll buy you some shoes on clearance."

"Clearance for you is a $400 pair of shoes. Clearance for me is, Payless Shoes."

"I was thinking we should go to the spa here after lunch. I already checked it out. We can get a massage," said Melanie as she turned on the shower.

"That sounds wonderful."

The ladies left 45 minutes later to catch a limo to the shopping district.

The sun was starting to peek through the clouds as the ladies got out of the limo right in front of Barney's New York. Samantha could smell Chanel perfume as the glass doors opened. The place was exquisite with its marble floors and crystal chandeliers. There was a champagne bar in the shoe department.

"Are you supposed to celebrate after buying expensive shoes or, get drunk and forget you ever bought them?" Melanie said as she tried on a pair of beautiful silver shoes. She didn't need another pair. She already has over ten pairs in her closet back home. Samantha sat on a chair and watched Melanie in amazement. A nice gentleman in a tuxedo brought champagne for both of them.

"Mel, this tastes expensive."

"It is. It's French. Enjoy!" Melanie admired her sexy feet in an ivory peep-toe pump.

Samantha admired a pair of gray suede ankle boots on the clearance rack. They were just her size and softer than toilet paper. She looked at the sole of the boot, $250. She put them back on the rack and Melanie grabbed them and put them next to her purse. "You're not leaving here empty handed. I know you want them. I'm going to buy them for you. Consider it an early birthday present."

"My birthday isn't for another five months."

"I don't care."

They finished their champagne and Melanie paid for the shoes and left a 50-dollar bill in the tip jar at the champagne bar. They proceeded to the makeup counter and they noticed a pianist playing a grand piano surrounded by red velvet ropes. Samantha received a text from Maria asking to call her.

"After looking at makeup we should find the restroom so I can call Maria."

"Alright. Is she ok?"

"I'm not sure."

"I have to call Bruno also. He just sent me a text."

The ladies bought lipstick and nail polish and went to the Ladies Lounge where there was a Spritzer lady and another one handing out towels to women using the sink. They sat down on a powder-blue velvet sofa to call their friends. Maria was upset and needed to talk to someone. She said that someone in her AA group fell off the wagon and drove drunk into a tree and was killed. Dr. King and Juan are at home with Maria and they are planning a memorial service for the end of the week.

Bruno was happy to hear from the ladies and told them where to go for lunch. They arrived at the restaurant 40 minutes later and were seated immediately. They ordered a large bottle of sparkling water and two orders of the Zebra Ravioli. Samantha used her smart phone to send flowers to Maria. Margaret was able to take over the jewelry store until after the memorial service.

The ladies arrived back at the hotel and dropped off their bags at the room and put on their terry cloth robes and went straight to the spa. They were able to get a full 2-hour treatment plus time in the sauna. They decided on room service for dinner. The ladies were leaving in the morning for the West coast and Samantha couldn't wait to spend time with Maria. She didn't think much about Bruno but he was understanding and supportive.

The next morning, the limo took the ladies to the airport and they decided to book the same flight so Melanie can also be with Maria for a couple of days before going home to Vegas. The ladies sat in first class and they were immediately greeted with champagne. Melanie fell asleep and Samantha got on her laptop to email Dr. King. She was feeling anxious and wanted an appointment this week. She also emailed Bruno so he can make arrangements to fly to Santa Barbara to be with everyone in a couple of days. Samantha wanted to go straight to Maria's house with Melanie as soon as they landed.

It seemed like such a short flight and Melanie slept the whole way. They landed and went to baggage claim and then went to the employee parking lot to retrieve Samantha's car.

The ladies arrived at Maria's house and Juan answered the door with Billy behind him. They were writing music together and Juan had a silver tray of hot tea he was taking upstairs and the ladies followed.

"Babe, you have company." Maria was happy to see them both. She was wearing mint silk pajamas and looked like she hadn't stepped out of the room all day and it was 3:30pm.

"You'll have to excuse me. I'm a little out of it. I will get myself together soon. There is a meeting at 6:00 and I plan to be there. Margaret will probably go with me."

"If you need us to go, we can also attend and be supportive."

"Only if you want to," said Maria. Samantha changed the subject without intention.

"My break-up went too smoothly and now I feel angry for some reason. It wasn't what I expected and I made an appointment with Dr. King to resolve some issues."

"I know the feeling," said Maria as she sipped her tea.

"Do you want to tell us what happened?" asked Melanie.

"There's not much to tell." Maria looked sad as she told the story. "Her name was Joanne and she was sober six months and went out on a date with a regular guy. She never bothered to tell him about her sobriety and he bought her a few drinks and the rest is history. It's not his fault. He had no idea."

"Where did she meet this man?" asked Melanie.

"A dating website."

"That figures. They're all sleazy. What ever happened to the days where you meet a man in a club and you marry him a month later?" Melanie smiled to break the ice.

"You got lucky," said Samantha.

A couple of hours later they all met at the university for an AA meeting and the place was packed. Word got around fast that

Joanne had passed away. It seemed more of a memorial service than a meeting.

The leader of the group spoke. "We lost one of our own today at a young age. She is with the angels in heaven watching over us and keeping us safe from danger. Joanne will be missed." The meeting lasted 90 minutes and then the friends went to Paradise Café, including Billy. They ate dinner and spoke openly about their lives and Dr. Gwen King spent most of the time at the table. No one knew Joanne well enough to say much but she did buy some jewelry from Maria over the holidays and Maria wished she would have spent time with her. This made her think of Jack and how short life can be. Dr. King brought an apple pie to the table for dessert and that made everyone smile and Billy took the spatula and served everyone. Bruno sent Samantha a text and wanted to fly out tomorrow night and she agreed. Her appointment with Dr. King was in the early afternoon so the timing would be right. Billy spent one more night at Juan and Maria's house to finish writing songs and he would be on the road for three weeks touring.

Samantha arrived 10 minutes early to her appointment and she pressed the button in the waiting room to let Dr. King know she was there. A few minutes later the doctor let her in.

"Have a seat. How have you been? It's been a few weeks since our last session."

"I know. My schedule has been crazy. I feel like I'm on a roller coaster. I have good days and bad days." Samantha had tears in her eyes.

"Tell me what's that like? You might want to start taking the meds I suggested before."

"I have a great life but I get these crying spells for no reason and then I get angry right afterwards."

"How often?" Dr. King started taking notes.

"About three times a week."

"How long do these episodes last?"

"I would say an hour; sometimes more."

The doctor looked concerned.

"Do you feel as though you are working too much? Do you need time off?"

"No. My job keeps me focused but when I was flying home from New York City I had chest pains but I wasn't working. It was a personal trip. I had just broken up with Jay. I mentioned him before; that no good son of a bitch. We had a civil break up and very few tears but now I'm just pissed!"

"You are going through the grieving process and this can take a few weeks." Dr. King handed her the box of tissue and wrote a prescription for medication.

"I know I'll feel better tonight. Bruno is coming over and he treats me so well. I'll make sure to take this one slow. I do need time to myself."

"Are you worried about your biological clock? Does that matter to you now?"

"I'm in my late 30's and it hasn't concerned me. I can live without children and if I get the urge, I can adopt."

Dr. King and Samantha finished their session with a hug and agreed to see each other again in two weeks.

When Samantha got home, she noticed her friends on Margaret's balcony being sophisticated ladies drinking wine and Maria drinking iced tea. The sun was going down and everyone was relaxed. Billy and Juan were still at Maria's house and Maria didn't want to be in the way. They were almost finished working.

"Samantha! Come join us," said Margaret.

"You guys are partying without me huh," Samantha said jokingly. "Bruno will be here in two hours so I do have time for a glass of wine."

"How was your session?" asked Maria.

"I'm going to start on anti-depressants as soon as possible. I haven't been myself lately."

"I don't blame you. I've been taking them for years and I feel great," said Melanie as she sipped her wine.

"Of course, you have Ms. Happy," replied Samantha.

Bruno arrived on time and Samantha was in the kitchen making dinner.

"I bought your favorite salad dressing. I'm surprised Italian isn't your favorite."

"I guess I have different taste buds. Poppy seed has always been my favorite. Hey, I heard someone passed away. Who was that?"

"Someone in AA that we don't know and Maria barely knew her either. The funeral is Wednesday and I'll be working. I'll be in Seattle and then Vegas. I can officially stay with you now. I'm unattached."

"Are you now?" Bruno hugged and kissed Samantha and she poured him a drink.

CHAPTER 17

Maria was walking away from the Mission gravesite with Juan and she felt nauseous. Most of the AA group was at the funeral of the deceased showing their support. Billy was on tour, Bruno, Samantha, and Melanie were out of state and Margaret was watching the jewelry store. They went to Paradise Café for lunch and most of the mourners were there and Dr. King came to their table.

"Hello, how are you guys doing? I'm glad you showed your support."

"Of course. We know what this is all about."

"Not to change the subject, I wanted you two to hear it from me first. I'm thinking about selling the restaurant."

"What?! You can't do that! Why?" Asked Maria.

"It's a lot of work and I'm taking on another class at the university. I wouldn't be here to run things."

"What about a silent partner?" suggested Juan.

"No, it's all or nothing. This won't happen until Spring so let's keep it quiet until then."

"This is a landmark. I'd hate to see it go."

"I know, so let's talk about happy things now; like wedding dress shopping."

"As soon as Samantha comes back from Vegas, I will ask her to be my maid-of-honor."

"She will be so thrilled!"

The couple ate their deviled eggs and finished their cranberry juice and mingled with the rest of the crowd.

It was a rainy and windy afternoon so Samantha turned on the heater and invited Maria to come over and watch a movie. Samantha had the next two days off and Bruno and Melanie were in Vegas and Margaret was minding the shop. Maria came over and they made hot coco and picked an old classic from the pile of DVD's. 'The Graduate'. Before they started the movie, Maria asked Samantha to be maid-of-honor at her wedding. It was such a surprise. Samantha thought she would pick someone AA or choose Dr. Gwen King. She happily accepted and couldn't wait to go dress shopping or at least look through magazines to get an idea of Maria's taste for fashion.

"Since Juan bought the ring in Las Vegas, wouldn't you like to get the dress there also? Do we need Mel's help?"

"I wouldn't mind getting it there but Mel has expensive taste and I want to keep this simple," replied Maria.

"Have you set a date yet?"

"We were thinking, late May and we want a garden wedding. No more than 60 or 70 people."

"That's small for a musician but in a way it's more personal and intimate. I like that idea," said Samantha as she started the movie.

The wheels of the plane hit the runway and Samantha was glad to be in Las Vegas for a 3-day layover. This was her second home. She kept clothes at Melanie's house and know she will be staying at Bruno's. It's ironic that Melanie doesn't have a boyfriend but many male friends. She's been a widow for quite some time and maybe wants to keep it that way. She has interesting male friends that want to settle down but she is too wealthy and they would have to sign a pre-nup. It's better to keep life simple with her charities.

Bruno picked up Samantha at the airport and this time Melanie was cooking at Bruno's house. She makes great Chicken Casserole. 'The Beach Boys' were playing on the XM radio in the kitchen when they walked in.

"Are we listening to surf music in Vegas? That's a first," said Bruno.

"The music helped with my acrimonious behavior and cheered me up," said Melanie as she hugged the both of them.

"Were you feeling blue?" asked Samantha.

"I didn't meet my goal at the charity luncheon today. Enough about me. How are both of you?"

"I can use a glass of wine," said Samantha as Melanie poured the Chardonnay.

Bruno's phone rang. "Excuse me ladies. I have to take this." Bruno stepped out to the patio to take the call and spoke in Italian.

"It must be important. He's not speaking English," said Melanie.

"I've never heard him speak Italian before. It has to be a family member."

"Of course." Melanie smirked.

"Do you know something?"

"I know enough. I've known Bruno for almost 20 years. I can tell when there's a problem. I just pretend not to know. I have big ears. It's probably his cousin, Chipper. He called earlier."

"He has a cousin named Chipper?"

"It's just a nick name. He put a rat through a wood chipper years ago."

"We're not talking about a rodent, are we?"

"I don't know anything and you didn't hear it from me."

"Are you sure it is safe for me to date him?"

"Yes. He's clean but his family is still in the Mafia. His family is getting smaller because they are slowly getting out of 'the life'. He's friends with the Feds and the Cops. He's sort of a middle-man."

"Like a double agent?"

"More like a messenger. He's coming inside now. Drink your wine."

"Sorry about that. Family business. I won't be taking any more calls today. You have my full attention."

Melanie poured a glass of wine for Bruno and he stared at the embellishments on the mantel above the fireplace. Samantha quickly changed the subject.

"Maria asked me to be maid-of-honor at her wedding and we'll be dress shopping very soon."

"Oh, that's terrific! Did she set a date?" asked Melanie.

"She said late May. She wants a garden wedding; probably at her house, I assume."

A Beatles song came on the radio. "Oh yes, this song takes me back," said Bruno as he served the casserole.

Bruno was a few years older than the ladies and he often told stories about his childhood in New Jersey. He kept them entertained until Melanie left at 11:00pm. The candles were still flickering with the breeze coming through the windows. Samantha began cleaning the kitchen in her bare feet and still had her uniform skirt on and a camisole. Her blouse was hanging over a chair and Bruno came over to load the dishwasher. Bruno lived in a newer development similar to Melanie's but four miles away. His home was larger with a massive wall around the property and cameras in every hidden corner. He enjoyed his privacy and also liked to entertain and even agreed to host a charity event for Melanie here on the property next month.

The couple went upstairs to get ready for bed. Samantha put on her silk robe and washed her face and looked in the mirror and saw the reflection in the background of Bruno taking his gun out of a holster on his calf. This worried Samantha and thought there might be trouble at the club.

"Honey, what time are you getting up in the morning?" asked Samantha.

"Oh, it depends. Do you want breakfast here or do you want to go out?"

"Tomorrow's Friday. Do you work?"

"I'll stop by work in the afternoon to check on things. I'll be gone for a couple of hours."

"Let's stay in then." Samantha finished putting night cream on her face and they both went to bed and slept soundly.

Samantha woke up to a rose and a note in the bathroom that read, '*I had to leave early for work honey. The coffee is ready. I'll be back soon.*' She didn't realize it was almost noon and she had slept over 10 hours. She went downstairs for coffee and bagels and texted Maria. Maria was at her jewelry store browsing through bridal magazines. She saw so many lovely dresses and it was difficult to decide on a style but she did agree to buy the dress in Las Vegas. Melanie could pull some strings at one of the shops so she started looking at air fare for next weekend. Melanie wanted Samantha and Maria to stay at her home and make it a girl's weekend. Margaret had to stay in Santa Barbara and mind the store. Bruno texted Samantha and said he would be home by 2pm so she went upstairs to take a long bath and read a book.

Bruno pulled in the driveway at 1:55pm and put his car in the garage and took the Italian food out of the back seat. He purchased lasagna, spaghetti, and garlic bread. There was enough food for six people. He wanted leftovers in case Melanie came over. Samantha welcomed him with a kiss and a glass of Chianti.

"How was your day?" asked Samantha.

"I had a meeting and did paper work. I also heard Dr. King is selling Paradise Café."

"What!? That place has been there forever. My father helped open that place back in the day. If someone buys it, they'll probably tear it down and put something else there."

"Not if I buy it."

"Can you do that? Do you have time to run another business?"

"I'll get a partner to run it."

"Ok, that sounds reasonable." Samantha changed the subject. "Do you want Mel to come over and help us eat all of this food?"

"Sure, give her a call. I'm going upstairs to change," said Bruno as he put down his glass of wine.

Melanie was nearby running errands and showed up ten minutes later. She kept an extra swimsuit in her trunk in case she gets invited to swim somewhere and this was the perfect occasion. The three friends enjoyed their food and sat in the hot tub for 45 minutes and then moved over to the large pool for more conversation. After a while, they sat on the patio and had dessert and coffee.

"I received an email from Dr. Gwen King and it said she is selling Paradise Café and wants to know if I'm interested in buying it," said Melanie.

"She sent me the same email," replied Bruno. "Are you going to make her an offer? You don't own any other property and it would be a good investment. You can afford it."

"Wait. Bruno, I thought you wanted to invest in it. The two of you should talk it over. You can become business partners. Mel, you can also buy a beach house and live in Santa Barbara full time."

"It's a lot to process at the moment. I will sleep on it," replied Melanie as she sat back in the patio chair and sipped her Cappuccino.

"Well ladies, I need to change the subject. I want to share something with both of you in confidence. The two of you are my closest friends so I should tell you I'm helping my cousin 'Chipper' get out of *The Life*. He confided in me and the Feds and he's going into the

Witness Protection Program and taking on a new identity. It's getting too dangerous for him to continue with the MOB."

"This night keeps getting better as we sit here," said Melanie

"Wait a second. If he joins Witness Protection, won't that mean he can't talk to you?" asked Samantha.

"Not exactly. I work with the Feds all of the time. I can help transform him and he can hide out here until things settle down and then take it from there."

"It's not too dangerous, is it?" asked Samantha.

"Not really. This place is very safe. Why do you think I have all of this security and a panic room and two pistols? To keep the Mafia out. This isn't the first time I've done this. I helped someone a couple of years ago."

"He sure did, Sam. I remember," said Melanie.

"I transformed a buddy and now he is working in Utah under a different name."

"When will you talk to Chipper again?"

"The day after tomorrow. Right after you leave, I will concentrate on that and you probably won't see me for a month."

"I guess I'll pick up extra shifts and hang out with friends. I'll be fine. This sounds important."

"It really is. I get joy out of helping other people."

Time flew by and it was almost time for bed so Melanie went home and Samantha and Bruno had a snack and went upstairs to make love. The next day they spent time shopping, eating and going to the movies. Samantha flew back home the following day. She knew being without Bruno for a month would be difficult but it was for a good cause.

CHAPTER 18

Maria had finally set a date for her wedding. May 30, 2011. She had two months to find a dress with the help of Melanie. She just landed in Las Vegas with Samantha and they were meeting Melanie at a bridal show. One of Melanie's drivers picked them up at the airport in a limo and drove them straight to Macy's Fashion Square. This was a formal event with top designers so the both of them wore business suits. Maria was in a black suit and Samantha in a blue suit; both of them wearing white silk blouses.

"Thank you for lending me this suit, Sam. I've never worn a suit before. I look like a lawyer."

"You look great and I'm sure there are plenty of lawyers at this event. You have to be a millionaire to get in to this place."

"We are not millionaires."

"No, but Melanie is and you will be also after you get married. Juan is a wealthy musician."

"Where is Mel meeting us? Is she meeting us on the sidewalk?"

"Yes. We are almost there. The driver is going to turn around and drop us off at the red carpet."

"There's a red carpet? This is fancy."

"Only the best for my girl."

"Oh my—Look at that banner!"

There was a huge banner in pastel blue that said, *Macy's Spring Bridal Show* and the was a giant white sand dollar on it. "Was that Mel's idea?"

"I'm sure she pulled some strings," said Samantha as she put down her sparkling water and got out of the car with the help of the driver. Samantha helped Maria out of the vehicle and there were many photographers taking photos of designers getting out of their cars and they quietly followed Vera Wang to the glass doors where Melanie was standing.

"I should have known you two would follow someone famous," said Melanie as she did a double kiss on both cheeks and put the lanyards around their necks.

"It wasn't on purpose. We just happened to be behind her."

"Don't take these off." Melanie was referring to the lanyards. "These are the passes to all of the events. Let's go to the bar first. We need drinks. Bruno is holding our seats at the Versace Runway. The show starts in 15 minutes." The ladies were excited to be there. Maria's eyes were wide open as though she were in shock and then she smiled and stared at the models walking by. Melanie put a bottle of Pellegrino sparkling water into her hand and it didn't even phase her. The ladies walked carefully up the stairs and Maria looked back at the crowded lobby.

"This is so amazing! I can't believe it. Is that Ralph Lauren?"

"Probably."

They reached the row of seats and Bruno stood up and waved. He gave the ladies a double European kiss on both cheeks.

"It feels like I haven't seen you in a long time," said Samantha.

"It's been a few weeks. Thank God for Skype."

The ladies sat down and the music started and the lights went dim. One model came out in a glamorous gown and then another followed. There were many flashes from photographers and Maria was on the edge of her seat clenching her drink. This was her first fashion show.

"Sugar, is this your first fashion show?" asked Melanie.

"Yes."

"Why didn't you say so? I get tickets thrown at me all of the time and I barely have time to go."

"There's a shocker." Bruno winked.

"I can't help it if I'm popular."

This show lasted 35 minutes and the group got up and went to another room with another runway. This time they went to see Vera Wang, Donna Karen, and Valentino.

Time went by and they needed a break to get lunch. Luckily, there was a café in the building serving traditional American and French cuisine. Maria ordered fish and chips and the others ordered club sandwiches.

"Have you seen a gown that you like?" asked Bruno.

"I have my eye on a Vera Wang gown. It's a simple slip dress with a V-neck and lace. I can't get it out of my mind."

"Then, that's the one honey. You keep thinking about it. You'll try it on and see how it looks on you. If you love it, I will give the associate my credit card and off we go. I have a private seamstress that will come to my house," said Melanie as she sipped more champagne.

"Are you out of your mind? I can't let you pay for it."

"It's my wedding present to you."

"It's $6,000!"

"So, what?"

"Well, all I can say is thank you. I can't believe I have such great friends." Maria had tears in her eyes.

They finished their lunch and went to one more show before Maria tried on the gown she liked. The gown fit perfectly except for the length. It was a little long but that was an easy fix. She put on her shoes and the female allies stood back with their faces lit up. Melanie brought out two veils and Maria picked the longer one.

"I'm paying for the veil. No arguments," said Samantha.

"I don't have the energy to argue so I'll pay for dinner tonight," replied Maria as a tear rolled down her cheek.

"It's a done deal." Melanie handed the associate her black American Express card and Samantha handed over her Visa.

Bruno was outside smoking a cigar with a designer he didn't recognize. The ladies came out and Bruno introduced the fellow to the ladies.

"This is Tom. Tom, this is my girlfriend Samantha, and my two friends, Maria and Mel." Tom kissed the back of their hands and excused himself.

"I better get back inside. My girls are almost finished." He put out his cigar with a smile and went back inside. The women stared in shock until they couldn't see him anymore.

"What's wrong with you ladies? Was he *that* good looking?"

"You don't know who that was, do you?" said Melanie.

"No, just some nice guy."

"That was Tommy Hilfiger!"

"No way."

"Yes way!" Maria and Samantha said in unison.

"Well, I just had a smoke with Tommy Hilfiger." Bruno smiled. "Where to now, ladies?"

"Do you want to go to my house?" suggested Melanie.

"That sounds good because I still have a house guest at my place," replied Bruno.

Maria and Samantha were spending two nights at Melanie's house and Maria was excited. She had never seen Melanie's house except in photographs and she knew it would be beautiful and glamorous.

Traffic was heavy but Bruno didn't mind. He had three classy ladies in his SUV and they all talked about the bridal show and how great it was. Maria couldn't wait to show Margaret the gown. Margaret had to keep an eye on the jewelry store so she couldn't attend the show.

They finally arrived at the house and Samantha looked at the take-out menus. They decided to have Chinese food delivered. Maria and Juan were texting back and forth and he was happy that Maria was having such a good time. Melanie showed Maria her jewelry collection and wanted Maria to take some pearls.

"These are lovely," said Maria while trying on a strand of pearls with matching earrings and bracelet.

"You can have these to keep."

"Are you serious?"

"I have too much jewelry. I bought that set years ago at Tiffany and I haven't worn them in years. They are yours now."

"Oh my… Thank you."

"The food arrived and Maria paid the delivery man and gave him a nice tip. Bruno poured iced tea for everyone and Melanie spoke about Paradise Café.

"Dr. King made me an offer on the club yesterday and it looks like I'm going to buy it," she said with enthusiasm.

"That's fantastic!" said Samantha.

"I'm so happy. I can't believe it," said Maria.

"Do you need a partner?" asked Bruno.

"Yes, I do. Would you like to be a silent partner?"

"I would. What's the cost?"

"I'm going to pay 2.5 million."

"That's cheap. You're getting a good deal," said Bruno.

"We should arrange to fly there next week to sign papers and talk about remodeling."

After everyone ate, Samantha and Bruno went out to the patio.

"Do you mind if I ask about Chipper?"

"Not at all. He's recovering nicely and he is leaving next week for Utah. He'll be safe there and I'll check on him periodically."

"It's nice what you're doing. You're like an angel with a bad-ass demeanor. No one is going to cross you."

"They have no reason to."

Bruno left early so the ladies could have a girl's night. He took some left-over rice and fortune cookies and went on his way.

"Maria, do you need some clothes? I'm going to clean my closet this week and give a lot to charity. Let's go upstairs and see what fits you," said Melanie.

"This is the happiest day of my life."

"This is nothing. Wait until the wedding shower. You're having one, right?" asked Samantha.

"Dr. King mentioned something at Paradise Café but she technically can't throw it since I'm her patient."

"Then we'll throw it for you at Paradise Café," said Melanie as she started taking expensive jeans off hangars. She made a large pile on the bed and Maria grabbed different outfits and put them against her body and looked in the mirror with a smile. The ladies had a great time for two hours talking and looking at clothes. It felt like high school.

The next morning, Maria woke up early to swim laps and make omelets and French toast. Samantha and Melanie came down and they ate on the patio.

"Where did you find the French Press? I forgot I had it,"

"It was in the cabinet with the fancy dishes."

Melanie had three sets of dishes and the fine China hasn't been used since she was married. It was a beautiful set of Noritake with gold leaf trim.

"We should sit in the hot tub before we go shopping," advised Samantha.

"I just had a thought. We are all close in age, including Margaret, and none of us have children," said Maria.

"I almost had one many years ago. I miscarried. I was in college and I wasn't serious with the guy so maybe it was for the best. I probably would have been a single mother and my life would be very different," said Melanie.

"That right. I remember that," said Samantha.

"It's never too late to adopt," said Maria.

"I have my children's charities and that seems to satisfy me for now but never say 'never'.

"I would like to adopt someday but I will leave that up to Juan and his crazy schedule."

"That sounds like a plan," said Samantha as she got up to clear the table.

The ladies sat in the hot tub for 20 minutes before getting ready.

"I might as well catch the flight with you two tomorrow. I want to sign those papers with Dr. King. I better let Margaret know I'm coming," said Melanie.

"You should buy a house in Santa Barbara if you're going to be running the club," advised Samantha.

"You're absolutely right. I'll call a realtor when I get there."

The sky was cloudy so Melanie pulled out three umbrellas from the hall closet as the ladies waited for the driver to pull the car around. They wore jeans with boots and the weather was 60 degrees. It was a nice day to shop and have lunch. Maria wasn't used to being this spoiled. She and Juan made a nice living but they don't have a personal driver; they only have a housekeeper that attends to their home once a week. Macy's was the first store they wanted to shop at and Melanie asked the driver to drop them off and pick them up in five hours.

"How often do you shop for clothes, Mel?" asked Maria.

"I shop every six months and I give my old clothes to Sam or donate them."

"No wonder Sam has such nice clothes."

"I share my dresses and blouses with Margaret. She doesn't fit into my pants because her hips are a little bigger than mine," said Samantha.

"I don't need to buy anything. You just gave me all of those clothes yesterday. Maybe I will buy a pair of loafers," said Maria.

The ladies looked at dresses and intimate apparel before going to the shoe department. Both Maria and Samantha texted their men to see what they were up to and Bruno agreed to go over to Melanie's house for dinner later. Juan was busy rehearsing and writing more music and would take in a museum later. Maria bought the COACH loafers she wanted and went to the cosmetic counter to buy an expensive sunscreen for Margaret and Coco Chanel for herself. JC Penny was having a sale on panty hose and that's exactly what Samantha needed for work. Samantha treated the ladies to a nice lunch at a restaurant in the mall. The time flew by and it was almost time to go home and Melanie noticed the rain.

"We need the rain. Vegas is so dry. I love this weather," said Melanie as she answered a text. "Oh, I just received a text from Dr. King. She is ready to promulgate the papers so Bruno and I can take over the club. He will be thrilled."

The next day, at the airport, Maria snuck over to the chocolate shop while Melanie and Samantha stayed at the gate before boarding the plane.

"Honey, why aren't we sitting in First Class?" asked Melanie.

"Because it's only a 55-minute flight. It's not worth the fuss. These are buddy passes."

"Alright. I hope there aren't any screaming babies on this flight."

"Put the ear phones on and listen to music."

"I need a drink."

"That figures. What's Maria doing?"

"She went to buy chocolate for Juan."

A man at the next gate was playing his guitar and it got Melanie's attention. "He sounds good. I wonder if he's famous."

"Go check him out. I'll wait here."

Maria came back and the gate attendant made the announcement for boarding. Melanie returned and the ladies boarded the plane.

"Was the guitarist someone you know?"

"No, but he's good. I took his name down and I'll Google him later."

"Maybe Juan knows him. What's his name?" asked Maria.

"Hank Silver."

The ladies were lucky to be sitting in the front of the plane so they can get their drinks first. Melanie ordered a 7 &7 and the other two ordered soda.

"If you move to Santa Barbara, what are you going to do with your three drivers?" asked Samantha.

"I will give them a nice pension. Trust me. I'll take care of them so they'll never have to work again. I'll keep the house in Vegas since it's paid for and my friends can stay there anytime."

"Do you think Bruno will sell his club, Samantha?"

"I think he will. He's helping another family member right now that is interested in the business."

The plane landed in sunny Santa Barbara and the ladies went straight to baggage claim.

It was two months until the wedding and Maria and Juan were picking out fine China for their China cabinet. It was going to be an intimate garden wedding and only 45 invitations went out. If everyone were to bring a plus-one, there will be close to 100 guests but this was not likely. Many musicians are single and Juan thinks they will show up without a date so they can meet new ladies. The close friends are already paired off except Melanie and she knows for sure that she will meet someone. She is ready to settle down and is looking forward to making Santa Barbara her new home again. Melanie remembers a wonderful time there at the university where she met Samantha. They had a business class together and both graduated together. Melanie continued on in the law program and danced at a club in Las Vegas every summer to pay her tuition.

Maria already hired a wedding planner and Melanie was eager to help pick out colors. Juan and Maria love lavender and there was plenty of it; right down to the flowers in the center pieces. Samantha will be wearing a lavender Nicole Miller dress and everyone else is encouraged to wear pastels. There will be swans in the fountain and Dr. King will initiate the ceremony. Doves will be released after the ceremony and Billy and the Band will be performing at the reception. Juan wrote his last check to the wedding planner and everything was set in stone. Maria was very happy with all of the plans and couldn't wait to marry the man of her dreams.

"That China cabinet looks amazing! Did you pick out the China set?" asked Melanie.

"Yes. I'll show you the catalog. It's vintage WATSON that was brought back from the 1950's. It's black with 24K gold leaf. It won't be used for the wedding. It doesn't match our theme but it's great for the holidays. I'll dress it up with red wine glasses and gold linen. My grandmother had the same set and it reminds me of Texas."

"I love it. It's different."

"Thank you. Margaret and Samantha will be here soon so we should steep the tea and get the sandwiches out."

The jewelry shop closed at 4pm on Sundays so Margaret can get over to the house and meet her friends there. Her life finally had meaning. She had quit smoking and was no longer on the patch. She drank less and still saw Gary when he was in town. The ladies were having a late tea party and this meant they would be having a late dinner when Juan got home. He was in Los Angeles heading home on his 90-mile drive. The doorbell rang and it was Samantha and Margaret with chips and guacamole.

"What is this? I knew you would bring snacks, you crazy girls," said Maria as she took the chips and put them in the kitchen.

"Something looks different. Oh, a China cabinet. Is this a wedding gift from Juan?" asked Samantha.

"Yes, it is and look at the China I picked out."

Suddenly, the subject changed to Margaret and Gary. "So, have you seen Gary lately?" asked Maria.

"Yes, we Skype. Does that count? He is coming here in a couple of days."

"If we are all here at the same time, we should meet at Paradise Café for lunch or dinner," suggested Samantha.

"That sounds like a plan. Now that the wedding plans are done, I can concentrate on looking at houses and maybe do some remodeling at Paradise Café," said Melanie.

"Bruno will be here in two days and he also wants to look at homes. The next few weeks will be busy for all of us," said Samantha as she bit into a cold sandwich.

"Gary might have connections with realtors in this area. He can probably suggest someone or you can use the same realtor Maria and Juan used," said Margaret as she took a sip of chamomile tea.

Bruno sat back in his office and took another puff of his cigar as a tear rolled down his cheek. It was April 15, 2011 and it was finally time to let go of the club. He had a few minutes before the new owner was to arrive to get the keys and the combination to the safe. At that time, he will gather all of the dancers for their monthly meeting and they had no idea that he sold the club and he would be leaving. He knew that they would be emotional and he wanted to leave peacefully and with dignity. He took another sip of his scotch and texted Chipper in Utah to see how things were. He was sure to use a secured cell phone the FEDs gave him to contact Chipper or Rusty. Little did everyone know; Rusty was coming back to Vegas to run the club and he made a complete transformation and his name is now John. He even had his tattoos removed so the dancers won't recognize him. He had to fake his own death three years ago to get out of *the life.* John walked into the club wearing glasses and a sharp-looking Armani suit. He had dropped 40 pounds and now wears blue contact lenses and he let his hair go gray. He walked slowly and took a look around and smiled at one of the dancers. One of the Federal Agents was at the bar disguised as a client and contacted Bruno. The agent spoke into his wrist. "He just walked in." Bruno stood up and buttoned his coat and drank the last bit of scotch before walking out of his office to meet John. Only the FEDs and Bruno knew who he really was. Rusty no longer exists. He was the captain of the notorious Mafia in New Jersey. He was no longer a dangerous man but could hold his own and would kill again if he had to. The employee meeting was set for 2pm so the music stopped and the light came on. The clients slowly filtered out as another FED manned the door and let the employees come in. The dancers, cocktail servers, and bartenders sat around in the lounge and Bruno asked one of the bartenders to open a few bottles of champagne to make a toast to the new owner. The federal agents stood outside so no one would come in.

"Did we get new security?" asked one of the dancers.

"No, these are undercover Cops to keep people out for this meeting. This will only take 30 minutes or so," said Bruno. The kitchen manager came out with appetizers and the meeting began.

"As most of you know, I've been here 15 years as the owner of this wonderful establishment. I've seen successful people come and go and for the most part, it's been quite wonderful. Las Vegas is such a great town and most of our clients come from old money. It's time for me to start a new chapter of my life so I sold the club recently and John will be taking over. This is John. He ran a casino in Utah and decided to give Las Vegas a try. I would like you to treat him with respect and I'm sure you all will. He's a nice guy but he's not as soft as I am." Bruno smiled and took a sip of champagne. He answered questions and tried to be as honest as possible. "John is the owner now and I just bought a club in Santa Barbara, CA. I'm actually co-owner. I have a partner. It's much different than this one. It's not exotic; it's more of a country club without the dues. Bands perform there and we hold wedding receptions, etc.… It's sophisticated and you can go to the website to read more about it."

"I take it, you are moving to California?" asked one of the bartenders.

"Yes, but I will be back to visit periodically. Let's eat and celebrate. This is a good thing." Some of the dancers did not look happy.

"Are the benefits going to change?" asked one dancer.

"What about pooling tips? What about our schedules?" asked another dancer.

"Nothing will change. We are only changing ownership. No one is being let go. We have a good staff here, from what I understand," replied John.

The rest of the meeting was calm and Bruno went into the office to clear his desk and waited for John. John came in and Bruno gave him the combination to the safe and removed his pistol and John put his pistol in. There were two security cameras in the office and seven cameras on the dance floor and bar. Bruno went out and shook hands with the bartenders and hugged a few of the dancers and went out to the parking lot and got into his car. He held on to the steering wheel and took a deep breath before going home to let the real estate agent in for the open house. His home was on the market for 3.2 million dollars. Bruno drove without any music; just the beating of his heart and the sound of his breathing. A tear rolled down his cheek. He will miss the club and his home but it was for the best. He was reinventing himself with a wonderful woman by his side.

Bruno pulled into his driveway and opened the security gate and noticed the 'For Sale' sign on the grass. The agent must have been by earlier but wasn't due for another 15 minutes. He backed his car into the garage and went inside and poured himself a glass of wine and poured olive oil on a plate to dip his bread. The house was spotless. The housekeeper spent extra time cleaning yesterday as well as the gardener and pool cleaner. He heard someone pull up and it was the agent with her client in a car behind her. Bruno opened the door and to his surprise, it was the real estate agent with an FBI agent named Tommy. Bruno has known Tommy as an acquaintance and he has seen him in the club.

"Hello Bruno. I didn't know you lived here."

"It's good to see you. I take it, you are shopping for a new home?"

"That's the plan. My wife is expecting so we need something bigger."

"Oh, good. You two know one another."

The woman slipped off her pumps and went to the dining room to put her things down and Bruno took Tommy to the kitchen for sparkling water and the woman followed. Tommy knows all about Bruno and how he helps people get out of the Mafia and into Witness Protection. They weren't here to talk business so Bruno had to keep it friendly.

"How do you two know each other?"

Bruno's phone vibrated in his pocket but he ignored it.

"Tommy's been by the club once or twice."

"Under cover I presume."

Bruno kept his answers short.

"Yes, something like that."

"Well, let's start outside, shall we?" suggested the realtor.

"There seems to be a lot of security here. I like that," said Tommy.

"You should see the panic room," said the realtor.

"Interesting," said Tommy as he grinned at Bruno.

They made their way inside and Bruno noticed the woman's phone light up with a call from Gary Jackson.

"Your phone is ringing," said Bruno.

"Oh, thank you. I need to take this." She excused herself and went to the other room.

"So, I heard you sold the club. Bold move. John is perfect for that place."

Bruno changed the subject. "Are you really interested in this big place? It's good for entertaining."

"Possibly."

"The realtor came back. "Ok, where were we?"

"Let's go to the basement. On second thought, we should go upstairs first. It's more elegant," suggested Bruno. "So, you know Gary Jackson? Sorry, I saw your caller ID. I met him on New Years Eve at a concert."

"We work for the same agency but he is a corporate agent. He sells hotels and casinos."

They went upstairs and checked out the four bedrooms. Each bedroom had its own elegant bathroom with a laundry chute leading to the basement.

"Have you started looking at homes in Santa Barbara?" asked Tommy.

"No. I would like to buy a piece of land and build my own but if there's a nice place that interests me, I will just add on and remodel it."

"That would be your best bet; that way you don't have to live in a temporary home while it's being built."

They made their way down to the living room and it was very modern and looked as though it had never been touched. Bruno has thrown a few parties but he has an excellent house keeper that brings her crew after every party to keep the place immaculate.

"Has the fire place ever been used?"

"Only once when we had that cold spell five years ago and lost electricity and the backup generator took two hours to kick in."

They made their way down to the basement that looked like a man cave with a bar and pool table. To the left of the bar was a door with a combination lock and this was the sound proof panic room which looked like a studio apartment. It had a bathroom with a shower, its own wine closet with the right temperature for wine, a gun rack for Bruno's rifles, and a small humidor with 50 cigars.

"Do the wine and cigars come with the house?"

"They do, but the rifles don't. I'll be taking those with me to California."

"I've never seen anything like this. You must be concerned about your safety," said the realtor.

"I grew up in a seedy neighborhood in Jersey, so---yeah."

"I have another appointment in 30 minutes. Do you mind if I take off and you two gentlemen can discuss things further?"

"That would be fine. We'll go to the backyard and sit on the patio," said Bruno.

The woman left and the men discussed business.

"I'm probably the only federal agent that has never seen this place. I heard it was incredible. My home now is vexatious and small. It's only a 3-bedroom, 2-bath house on the other side of town. So, tell me, have you ever used the panic room?"

"Not me personally but I put Chipper in there for a couple of days until things calmed down."

The men talked for another 45 minutes before Tommy left and promised to be in touch.

Samantha pulled into the parking lot at Paradise Café with Bruno in the passenger seat to meet everyone for lunch. The table in the corner was set for seven people and Melanie was already there with her apron on and cooking something in the kitchen. It was April 17, 2011 and Paradise Café was closed for remodeling and won't open back up until

June 5th. Most of the staff decided to stay on and only a few people had left to work at other restaurants. Construction was being done on the patio today so there was some hammering and drilling going on.

"Do you need help in the kitchen?"

"Everything is done but you can help bring out salads when everyone gets here. Maria just got out of her appointment so she'll be here in a few minutes."

Gary and Margaret just walked in and Juan followed behind.

"Wow! Look at you. You look like a chef. It smells good. What's on the menu?" asked Margaret while Bruno went to the bar to make drinks.

"We are having salad first, Chicken Piccata, and then Crème Brule for dessert."

"Where did you learn to cook?" asked Juan.

"Bruno, of course."

Maria walked in wearing a nice pastel dress.

"Who's minding the jewelry store?" asked Bruno as he handed beers to Juan and Gary.

"I closed it for three hours. I had too much to do today and Margaret is off for two days while Gary's in town." She put her purse down and kissed Juan. All of the ladies went into the kitchen to get bread and salads.

Juan turned on some1980's music. "Hey, is anyone free for golf tomorrow?"

"That's a great idea but I'm meeting a realtor tomorrow. Oh Gary, I forgot to tell you, the realtor in Las Vegas said she works for the same company that you work for," said Bruno.

"That's right. She mentioned it. Do you have to make any more trips to Vegas or is everything final?"

"Everything is final. My furniture is here in storage."

Melanie hung up her apron and everyone started on their salads.

"Gary, have you ever thought about buying a home here?" asked Melanie.

"Yes, but my work is in Vegas. I buy and sell casinos. If I go back to selling homes, I would be taking a huge pay cut. But, never say never. It's an option."

"The big day is coming up you two," said Samantha as she looked at Maria and Juan. They both smiled. "I'm marrying the woman of my dreams."

"Oh, thanks honey." Maria kissed Juan. "It's going to be perfect. Everything is all set."

Samantha and Melanie gathered the empty salad plates and went to the kitchen and Maria and Margaret followed.

"What time are you meeting the realtor?" asked Juan.

"9:00. We can play golf around 11. How about it, Gary?"

"Count me in."

Everyone enjoyed their chicken with mashed potatoes and Maria got up to make herself a Shirley Temple and get more beer for the boys. They took their time eating and bonding before having dessert.

"I think it's great that Dr. King will be performing the ceremony at your wedding," said Melanie.

"I know. It is special. Today was my last session with her and she is referring me to another doctor if I still need treatment but I don't think I will. I'm feeling well these days."

The friends enjoyed their time together before going home. Paradise Café is a magical place that keeps people happy.

The day was overcast and windy but that didn't stop Bruno and Samantha from looking at homes on this day of April in 2011. Bruno glanced online first and that narrowed his search to two homes, both mansions. The first home was near the mission and close to Juan and Maria's home. It was retro with a vintage feel to it. It had a sunken-in den with a circular fireplace, a small backyard and no panic room but one could be added to the home. Bruno would have to remodel and make a few changes. The palm tree in the front yard was a plus but not enough to pay 4 million dollars. The second home was a Spanish-style home with plenty of iron and had state-of-the-art cameras already installed and a panic room. It was two story with a large front and backyard and two swimming pools and a hot tub. There were two Italian fountains in the front yard and a rose garden in the side yard with a grapevine. This home was quite large and the asking price was 11 million and Bruno didn't want to go over 8 million but loved it so much that he was willing to negotiate.

"This place is amazing! Do you still need all of this security? It looks like Scarface used to live here," said Samantha as she snapped some photos with her smart phone.

"I'm still going to be working with the FBI. This place is perfect and it has a view of the ocean and you can see The Ritz Carlton. Do you like it? If I buy it, will you live with me?"

"Are you serious? Are you ready to take this relationship to the next level?"

"I've been ready for a long time. How about it?" Bruno smiled and kissed Samantha.

"It's a deal. What about my little beach house?"

"You can rent it out. It's up to you."

"Wow, I need to sit down for a minute."

The agent handed Samantha a bottle of Fiji water. "So many people love this home. A few celebrities have come to see it but I can't mention who. There is no pressure. It's fairly new."

"I don't need to think about it. Bruno is willing to negotiate the price." Samantha got on her phone and texted the ladies the news.

Bruno went to the bank and made the transaction before taking Samantha home and then he went straight to the golf course. Margaret had a bottle of champagne waiting on her balcony along with Melanie and Maria. Maria was drinking her usual diet soda with a lime and Samantha arrived to show photos of the beautiful home.

Bruno met the boys in the locker room of the golf course and Juan had already paid for all three of them. Gary and Juan didn't know exactly what Bruno did for a living but they knew it was important and Juan was happy to have him in Santa Barbara.

"Congratulations on your new home. When do you move in?" asked Juan as he tied his shoes.

"In two weeks. After your wedding, I'll be ready for a house warming party. Let's play some golf."

"I just received a text from Margaret. The girls are going to barbeque some burgers so we don't have to worry about dinner. We'll eat at Margaret's," said Gary.

The boys only played nine holes of golf so they can get home to eat. Gary won the game and Bruno came in second. They went to Margaret's house and had a wonderful dinner and drank beer by the fire pit.

CHAPTER 19

The sun peeked through the palm trees on the street where Maria and Juan lived. The breeze was a perfect touch to celebrate their nuptials and the front yard was decorated with silver streamers and helium balloons. It was May 30, 2011. Guests were starting to arrive and the catering team and butler showed them to the glamorous backyard. The friends were upstairs getting ready and the men were in a guest room with Juan drinking champagne and getting dressed while the ladies were in the master bedroom. Margaret and Melanie had on lavender chiffon dresses cut to the knee and Samantha had on the same except hers was long. Melanie applied the finishing touches of makeup to Maria's face and she looked stunning. Maria was ready to put her gown on and she couldn't stop smiling.

"Do you feel nervous Maria?" asked Samantha.

"Not at all. This is the happiest day of my life."

"I'm glad you feel calm because I'm a fucking wreck! My stomach is in knots."

"Why? You don't look like you're nervous."

"I want everything to go well. You deserve it."

"Thank you. It will. It's already perfect."

More guests arrived and they followed the harp music to the back-yard. There was a lovely lady playing the harp and there were swans in the fountain. There were rows of white folding chairs with satin lavender ribbons enough to seat 45 people. The bartender was set up on the patio wearing a white suit serving lavender martinis to the guests. Dr. King was under the floral arch looking over her notes on matrimony while the guests started to seat themselves. The banquet tables were set off to the left side of the fountain with beautiful center pieces. The rows of chairs were on top of the wooden dancefloor and will be removed after the ceremony.

Margaret heard a knock on the door.

"Hi ladies. We're heading downstairs now. We'll see you in a few minutes," said Bruno.

"Ok, we are ready," said Margaret. The ladies waited two minutes before going down. The men wore black tuxedos except Juan; he had a gray tuxedo. Billy Taylor was the Best Man standing by Juan under the archway while Gary and Bruno helped seat the rest of the guests. Melanie and Margaret went straight to the arch to join the gentlemen while Samantha stayed with Maria to straighten her short train and long vail before going up. Maria was on the patio ready to proceed and holding her cascade bouquet of white and sterling roses. The musician playing the harp changed to a wedding march song and Maria slowly walked down the white carpet covered in sterling rose petals. She chose to walk alone in Jack's memory. It's what he would have wanted since he couldn't be there to give her away. She reached the arch and turned to Juan and they both smiled in bliss.

"Dearly beloved, we are gathered here today in holy matrimony. Juan and Maria have decided to share their live together uniting as one with God, friends, and family. Marriage is an important occasion bringing two people together as best friends, lovers, husband and wife. The lovely couple have written their own vows. Juan, why don't you begin."

Juan held Maria's hands in his. "Maria, when I first met you, I knew you were special. You were fragile, kind, giving, and a good friend to everyone around you. You became a part of everyone's lives. You are beautiful inside and out and I look forward to spending the rest of my life with you."

Maria had tears in her eyes as she was focused on Juan. "Juan, you are a handsome and kind man. You picked up the pieces of my life when I was most vulnerable. I'm excited to be you wife and spend the rest of my life with you."

They were given the rings from Billy and Samantha and they slipped them on each other's fingers.

"By the power invested in me and the state of California, you may now kiss the bride."

Juan and Maria kissed passionately and the guests smiled and clapped.

"Let's welcome Mr. and Mrs. Juan Compra."

The bride and groom both turned around and waved to the guests and the servers poured champagne for everyone. This was not a traditional wedding so Maria planned on giving her bouquet to Samantha for good luck after posing for photos. The photos took 35 minutes to take and the last photo was taken at the Bridal Table with Maria bent over kissing the glass center piece with sand, seashells, and a sand dollar inside and Juan looking on in peaceful harmony. It was like kissing Jack on the cheek and having him look over Maria and blessing their marriage. This black and white photo will be blown up very large to cover the wall above the sofa in the living room. The bridal party went upstairs to freshen up while the guests drank and the servers passed out appetizers. Samantha helped Maria out of her dress so she can use the bathroom and Melanie and Margaret took photos of each other with their cell phones and drank champagne.

"This bouquet is for you, Sam. You've been such a gem and you deserve to have it."

Maria handed the bouquet to Samantha and hugged her. The bouquet was a cascade of beautiful silk flowers that will last a lifetime. Samantha put it next to her purse and the ladies went downstairs to meet their men and everyone clapped as Juan and Maria went outside. Billy got a bite to eat and set up his band by the dance floor and Juan and Maria went through the buffet line. Everyone soon followed. Billy said a few nice words as he toasted the bride and groom and Samantha took over the microphone to say nice things about Maria. The bride and groom finished eating and then had their first dance while 'Billy and The Band' sang a romantic song.

Everyone had a great time as the sun dipped between the palm trees and the reception came to a close after 7pm. Maria went upstairs to change into comfortable clothes. She opened the window in the guest bathroom and a strong breeze came through and a butterfly landed on the counter. She thought this might be good luck. Maria removed her veil and put it on the hook on the wall and smiled at her reflection in the mirror and turned to admire the welkin.

CHAPTER 20

Four months had gone by, the tourists had gone home, and the students had taken over Santa Barbara. It was a busy Summer for Melanie and Bruno at Paradise Café and Samantha was on a 2-day layover in Chicago. The date was September 11, 2011 and she was watching the 10-year anniversary of 9-11 on TV and couldn't believe it had been 10 years already and she knew exactly what she was doing at that exact moment. She and Melanie were just waking up on the West coast in her beach house on that sad morning in 2001. The world had changed forever.

Maria and Juan walked into Paradise Café and everything was decorated in patriotic form. There was a banner above the stage where Billy was playing the piano which read, 'We Will Never Forget 9-11-01'. Billy played some patriotic songs and then some slow songs in tribute to the soldiers that serve in the military. It was 5pm and it was already a full house with students and military members. Food and drinks were comped for military personnel and many of them wore their uniforms and they were on leave ready to be shipped out again in a couple of days.

In Chicago, Samantha went to a bar and grill in her hotel and sat at the bar with a martini and watched everything unfold on the news. She felt alone and sad until the bartender struck up a conversation with her and reminded her of Jack.

"Can you believe it been 10 years already? I'm Neil, by the way."

"Hello, I'm Sam. The world sure is different now."

"I take it, you are just passing through."

"Yes. I'm on a layover. I work for the airlines."

"How ironic. You must be a flight attendant."

"Lucky guess."

"I can tell by your beauty."

"Thank you."

"Also, I'm a psychology major so I pick up on things like that."

"That's a good field to be in. I have a friend who is a psychiatrist. She was my therapist before we became friends. Now, we are just friends."

Neil wiped down a wine glass and put it on the shelf. "I'm studying Criminal Psychology."

"That sounds intense."

"It's incredible; especially the way the world is today. My fiancé is a school teacher and she sees a lot of activity every day. Most of the kids are well-behaved but some are rotten and potential serial killers. I know that sounds extreme but look at all of these school shootings. The gunmen are honor students with high IQ's."

"This is true." Samantha took another sip of her martini while Neil poured a beer for a guest."

"So, what town are you from?" asked Neil.

"Santa Barbara, California."

"Oh, nice college town. I have some buddies that graduated from UCSB. So, you're not married? No ring?"

Samantha blushed. "I live with my boyfriend. I've never been married; maybe someday."

"What does your boyfriend do?"

"He has a government job with the FBI and he owns a café in the middle of town in Santa Barbara."

Samantha didn't want to give too much away. She didn't let on that the café was actually a night club and Bruno's family is in the mafia.

"Is he an agent?"

"No, a consultant."

"He sounds like a catch. Good for you."

Samantha finished her drink and excused herself to go upstairs. "I'll see you around," said Neil as he watched her exit the bar with her beautiful legs.

"She's what dreams are made of," said a patron.

"I hear you," said Neil with a smile.

Samantha woke up to a text from Maria.

'Please call me. I have great news!'

Samantha used the bathroom and splashed water on her face and made coffee before calling Maria.

"Hey, you. What's this great news you have? Are you adopting a baby?"

"No." Maria laughed. "Juan is nominated for a Grammy and he is performing at the Grammy's!"

"Oh my God! Are you serious? When?"

"In January. I'm so excited! I get to invite two guests. You and Bruno are invited!"

"Are you sure that's ok?"

"Yes. Juan said so."

"I'm so grateful. Thank you! Should I tell Bruno?"

"He already knows."

"Oh, good. I have a flight to catch. We'll talk when I get home this afternoon."

"Ok, sounds good. See you then."

"Bye."

Samantha poured her coffee and texted Bruno.

"We're going to the Grammy's!"

It was cloudy in the Windy City of Chicago when Samantha got out of the cab at the airport. She was looking forward to having a few days off with her man and seeing her friends. She went through security and went straight to the Sky Lounge to meet with the rest of her crew and drink a large coffee before boarding the plane. The pilot approached Samantha while she was checking email on her phone.

"This flight might be delayed for a while. There is fog in Santa Barbara and it's not safe to land. Have yourself some juice."

"Will do. Thank you."

Back in Santa Barbara, orders started coming in for the holidays at Maria's shop. Clientele were ordering a lot of jewelry online since she updated her website. Margaret was feeling overwhelmed and suggested she hire a temp even though it was still early in the season. People start shopping as early as October 1st. Maria agreed with Margaret and complimented her on her new look.

"You look good. Are you still jogging every morning? Your skin is glowing."

"Since I quit smoking, everything seems brighter and I have more energy. I also save money since I don't buy cigarettes any more. I spend the money on facials and I decided to try a little Botox also."

"You look amazing."

"Thank you. I want to look good for Gary."

"I'm buying you lunch today. Do you want me to bring you Chinese, or subs with salad?"

"You better make it subs and salad. Thanks."

"I hope you don't mind; I've invited Sam and Bruno to the Grammy's. We only have two extra tickets."

"I don't mind at all. Sam is your best friend and I would never break that bond. I'm curious to see what she will wear."

"Maybe she'll borrow a gown from Melanie, or Bruno will buy her one."

Samantha's plane finally got off the ground after being delayed two and a half hours. She was working first class and only three business men were in her section. One man on his laptop, another reading the newspaper, and another man with a gel sleeping mask on to reduce puffiness. This was an easy gig for the ride home and Bruno will be getting off work when she lands. Bruno wanted to leave work early so he can have a bubble bath ready for her. Their Jacuzzi bathtub heats itself to a nice temperature of 103. When Bruno was driving home, he received a call from a family member he hadn't spoken to in over 15 years. It was his notorious God Father whom Bruno was named after. It was ironic that he was listening to opera music on the stereo when the call came through and he didn't know who it was. A chill went up his spine when he realized who it was and he was in the neighborhood. The caller-ID was from a local number and Bruno senior was calling from a pay phone at the Santa Barbara airport.

Samantha's plane landed with ease and she helped some passengers exit the plane. She said good bye to the crew and took her rolling luggage through the terminal. She noticed a stocky man on a pay phone (pay phones were scarce in 2011 and the airport still had them) that resembled Bruno and she had to look twice to see who it was. He had the same built and the same receding hairline. She took a deep breath and kept on walking but he also noticed her staring at him and thought it was a flirtatious glance. He cut the call short and followed the slender flight attendant hoping they can share a cab. Samantha proceeded to the employee parking lot to her car and realized she was being followed. This time, he put on his sunglasses and she didn't know it was the same man that was on the pay phone. She began to walk faster not knowing she dropped her scarf. Bruno senior slowed down and tried not to startle her. He picked up her scarf and walked to her car as she was putting the luggage into her trunk.

"Excuse me, ma'am? You dropped your scarf."

Samantha turned around. "Oh, thank you. I didn't realize I dropped it. That was kind of you to bring it to me." She looked through his Prada glasses and realized it was the same man in the terminal.

"Well, I must be going. I need to catch the shuttle to my hotel."

Samantha smiled. "Yeah, I have to go too. My boyfriend is waiting for me." She accentuated the word '*boyfriend*' so he would move on.

He noticed her name tag before leaving. Samantha was driving home and Melanie called her on Bluetooth.

"Hi Sam. Are you home yet?"

"Almost. My flight was delayed. I'm driving home now."

"I heard that you and Bruno are going to the Grammy's. That's exciting! I'm also going."

"Of course, you are," Samantha replied sarcastically with a smile.

"Billy Taylor invited me and I'll be his plus-one."

"Oh, that's fantastic! Is he performing?"

"No, he's a presenter."

"Well, I'm almost home. I'll stop by Paradise Café tomorrow so we can catch up."

"Sounds good. See you then, bye."

"Bye, Mel."

Samantha pulled into her driveway and opened the garage to see Bruno putting tools away and smiling as Samantha got out of her convertible. Bruno was wearing a Ralph Lauren polo shirt and blue jeans.

"Hi doll." Bruno kissed her and took the suitcase out of the trunk.

"Hi. What are you up to?"

"I was just tightening a faucet in the panic room."

"Really? Are we having company soon?"

"Yes. Are you hungry?"

"Not yet."

"Good because your bath is ready and we can talk about what is happening."

"A bath sounds good right now."

Bruno senior arrived at The Ritz Carlton hotel and checked in under a different name. He paid cash for two nights and gave the front desk $2,000 for amenities. A federal agent waited for him by the elevator and took him to his room. He called Bruno and they agreed to meet the next morning.

"What are your plans for tomorrow?" asked Bruno as he rubbed a loofa on Samantha's back in the bath.

"I'm meeting Mel at Paradise Café for lunch. Will you be there?"

"I probably won't be there. I'm meeting someone at The Ritz Carlton tomorrow."

Bruno's opaque words left Samantha wondering what he was up to. "Anyone I know?"

"Actually, my Godfather is in town. I haven't seen him in many years and he needs my help."

"Is he a true Godfather or is he a Mafia Boss?" Samantha spoke directly to get a straight answer.

"He is, and he was a captain, not a Mob Boss. I owe him a lot. If it wasn't for him, I'd still be in the Mafia right now. He got me out of that life and sent me to Vegas and then we lost contact until recently."

"This sounds dangerous, Bruno. What's his name?"

"Bruno senior. I was named after him. He is twenty years older than me. He will be staying here along with the Feds so it will be safe. You don't have to worry."

Samantha had a puzzled look on her face as she remembered the gentleman at the airport.

"Did he fly in today? I saw a man today that resembled you. He was using a pay phone at the airport."

"That was probably him. He got rid of his cell phone so he can't be traced."

"Do I have to keep this to myself or does Mel know?"

"I will let her know. I can talk to her in code. She's used to that." Bruno changed the subject and they talked about Autumn and how the students had filled up the town and how busy Paradise Café was getting.

Thirty minutes later, Bruno went downstairs to start dinner.

Samantha came downstairs in silk pajamas and a clean face. "It smells good down here and my wine glass is empty."

"The Mahi is ready but first, we are having salad and bread sticks."

"Sounds delicious."

They decided to make it an early night. They were in bed by 8pm and watched a movie in bed and fell asleep at 10:30.

Bruno had just left Paradise Café before Samantha arrived there. She walked in and went to her usual table and Melanie took off her apron and asked the bartender to make drinks for the two of them.

"You have good timing. I just finished baking and I feel like I'm up to my eyeballs in flour."

"I'm so glad we are meeting for lunch. It's been a while."

"You just missed Bruno."

"I know. He has a meeting. Did he talk to you about our next visitor?"

"Yes, he did. How do you feel about that?"

"In Vegas, it was fine because we didn't live together. But now, it feels different. I have no say in what goes on. I know he is doing good work and the Feds are involved but there is so much secrecy and there is never any warning when we have visitors."

"At least there is a 48-hour gap before Bruno senior moves in. That gives you a chance to get used to the idea. He's supposed to move in soon."

"He looks like Bruno and his name is Bruno. What am I supposed to call him?" said Samantha in a frustrated voice.

"I'm sure they're discussing that right now. Let's decide on lunch. It'll get your mind off of things."

The ladies drank their wine and ate garlic bread until their Cobb Salads arrived.

"Do you have the next few days off?" asked Melanie.

"Yes, I do."

"Great. I want to look at houses and I want you to come with me."

Melanie opened her laptop and they browsed o few homes online. She wanted a 2-story modern home so she can entertain. Samantha received a text from Bruno asking her to be home by 8pm so they can discuss Bruno senior. She didn't respond and turned off her phone and made sure she would be home by 8:00.

Samantha decided to stop at Sand Dollar Jewelers at 6:30 to visit with Maria and Margaret, and Juan happened to be there also. They were ordering more men's jewelry for the display case. They decided on more gold crosses and Jewish Stars for the holidays. A beautiful platinum and turquoise cross were on display in the black velvet case for $700. That was a small price to pay for the clientele who shop here.

"Congratulations on your Grammy nomination, Juan," said Samantha.

"Thank you! It was unexpected but I've been working hard on my new album. It comes out in November."

"Fantastic! What's it called?"

"Moments. You're getting a signed copy as soon as they are delivered."

"Thank you."

"What's Bruno up to today?" asked Maria.

"He's in a meeting. We might have one of his relatives stay with us for a while."

"Sounds lovely."

"Yeah, what a treat," Samantha responded sarcastically.

It was September 13, 2011 and Samantha pulled her car into the garage at 7:35pm and Bruno was not home yet. She went to the kitchen and poured herself a glass of wine and turned on the TV. Bruno just texted her saying he was on his way home. He pulled into the garage and took a red rose from the passenger seat that he had bought at the hotel.

"Hi honey. How was your day?" asked Bruno.

"Is that rose for me?"

"Yes, of course."

"Thank you," Samantha said with a smile.

"How was lunch with Mel?" She's really working hard at the club."

"I know. She could use some extra help."

"Funny you should mention that." Bruno poured himself some wine. "I'm thinking of putting Bruno senior in the kitchen as a chef. He would be perfect. He used to run his own restaurant back home."

"Isn't he supposed to be in hiding?"

"I'm talking after the transformation. We don't have to do much; just some cosmetic surgery on his chin and he'll be wearing glasses from now on. He agreed to shave his head."

"When is he coming here?"

"Day after tomorrow. He's getting the procedure done in the morning. I'm taking him to the doctor. You look worried."

"I just want to be safe."

"We will have two Feds here at all times. One in front, and one in the backyard. This place is tighter than a prison."

"Yeah, tell me about it."

It began to rain as Melanie and Samantha pulled up to a big home near the botanical garden. The home was at the top of a hill further from town and the ocean was over four miles away. The home was very large and 100 years old. It was Spanish style with many trees and it had seven bedrooms and five bathrooms. They met the realtor at the front door and when she opened it, they noticed two fountains in the foyer; one on each side with Spanish tile and gold fish.

"This looks like a hotel lobby," mentioned Samantha.

"We can have great parties here," said Melanie.

One of the rooms had a hard-wood floor and vaulted ceiling with track lighting and a large painting of a woman without a blouse on, laying on her side with only a sheet covering her hips and abdomen. Her eyes were closed as though she was sleeping. Samantha thought it to be salacious.

"This room was an art gallery at one time. The artist owned this home and before he moved back to Spain, he sold all of his paintings except this one of his wife Marisol. He wanted to remember her this way; in perfect lighting. She broke his heart when she took her own life a couple of years back," explained the realtor.

"A tragic love story. It makes me want the house even more. I'm intrigued. If these walls could talk…"

"Are you sure you need something this big, Mel?" asked Samantha.

"It's so perfect." Melanie's eyes lit up like a kid in a candy store.

Samantha whispered to Melanie. "This house is a mansion. It's 8 million dollars!"

"Yeah, so what's your point? I'll pay 10 million if I have to. It feels right and it has an incredible vibe."

"It's probably haunted."

"Even better. I'll take it!" Melanie said to the agent.

"I'm so happy you picked this home. A celebrity looked at it yesterday but didn't make an offer. His loss. This house suits you. Let's go to my office and sign some papers."

Melanie's face lit up and she smiled all the way downtown while she was driving.

"That house is triple the size of your house in Vegas. I hope you know what you're doing. You're going to need staff."

"Oh, a cabana boy!"

Samantha turned her head to look away from Melanie. She didn't know what else to say.

It was a sunny afternoon at Maria and Juan's house while Maria finished stirring a glass pitcher of lemonade. All of the friends were there, including Billy Taylor and Margaret's boyfriend Gary, who happened to be in town. The patio table was set for eight and Juan finished cooking the steaks on the barbeque. Samantha and Melanie were by the fountain speaking softly.

"How are things at home, Sam?"

"Bruno senior hasn't come out of the panic room yet so I haven't officially met him. Oh, and he changed his name to Butch Jones so we can't call him Bruno anymore."

"I heard."

"It sounds like you know more than I do."

"The Feds were at the café yesterday talking with Bruno. I think that's when they decided a different name would be more sufficient. The Feds are pulling the strings. Bruno doesn't have much input. You should go easy on him. He's doing a good deed."

"I know. I'm just worried about our safety. Who knows how many people this man has killed. I feel like he has blood on his hands."

"I'm sure he is sorry and regrets his past and that's why he is in Witness Protection. Do the other girls know that you have a visitor?"

"Not yet. I'm not allowed to say anything. Bruno will take care of that."

"I'm sure he will. The Feds will tell him what to do."

Margaret and Gary walked toward the fountain with their drinks to join Samantha and Melanie.

"Hey, girls. Are you going to mingle with the rest of us?" asked Margaret.

"Of course. We were just talking shop," said Melanie.

"How is the wonder Paradise Café?" asked Gary.

"Busy and fun at the same time."

Juan put the platter of steaks on the table and Billy put a large bowl of mashed potatoes and a boat of gravy next to the steaks.

"Come on guys. It's time to eat!" shouted Billy.

The friends held hands at the table and closed their eyes as Billy led them in a short prayer.

God, thank you for bringing us together. We have a great love and bond between us. Thank you for this delicious food we are about to devour. And thank you for this great weather. We couldn't ask for more. Amen.

Everyone opened their eyes and began to pass the food around.

"Who has great news? Anyone?" asked Bruno.

"Oh, I do!" said Melanie. "I just bought a house."

Everyone clapped and cheered as Bruno held up his glass of wine.

"Well, cheers to you Mel." Said Bruno.

Melanie passed her iPad around the table so everyone could see photos of her new home.

"Oh my God, Mel! This is the Marisol Mansion!" said Juan in surprise.

"I suppose it is."

"This place is legendary! It's been vacant for years and it belonged to the famous Ricardo Sanchez."

"Do you know about him?"

"He's a Spanish artist and he lived there with his wife Marisol. He used to throw lavish parties and I was invited to one over 10 years ago. It was a glamorous Mascaraed Ball and I never saw Marisol's face behind her mask and rumor has it, she wasn't even there. She had locked herself in one of the rooms upstairs because she was suffering from depression and didn't want to come out. She had two miscarriages and the doctor told her that she couldn't bare children. She took her own life the next day after the ball. I don't know who the glamorous woman behind the mask was; maybe a friend, or her twin sister. Anyway, Ricardo named the mansion after her and he left six months later for Spain and never returned. The place is haunted. Marisol's ghost still lives there."

"How tragic! You never told me this story," said Maria.

"I thought everyone knew. Jack never told you?"

"No. I wish he would have. Mel, you better get a Medium in there with some sage."

"I will. There are a lot of haunted places in Santa Barbara. This is a very old town. Look how old the Mission is."

"So true," said Margaret.

Melanie took a look at her phone and saw that it was already October 1, 2011. She took a sip of her tea that she bought at Starbucks. She was admiring the view from her new backyard and she turned around and saw all of the boxes near the door that the movers had left. The antique furniture left behind by Ricardo, were covered with sheets and she heard the psychic/medium pull into the driveway in her old diesel Mercedes. Melanie opened the front door for her.

"Hello, Susan?"

"Yes. Are you Melanie?"

"Yes, so glad to meet you. Please come in. Do you need a beverage? I have diet soda."

"No thank you. I'm good."

"I'll give you a tour."

"I've always wanted to walk through this house. My friends will be jealous."

The both of them walked slowly into every room of the house. Susan examined every wall as if she was investigating a crime scene.

"Well, what do you think?" asked Melanie.

"I'm going to sage the house. Marisol's spirit is everywhere but she won't harm anyone. She is happy that you moved in. She was lonely.

You don't want to eliminate her. She needs to be here. Let me sage all of the rooms and then we will discuss what happens next."

"Do I need to leave?"

"No. Actually, I need you with me in case she starts to communicate."

Susan pulled something out of her tote bag that looked like a gray branch of some sort. She put her bag next to the fish fountain and lit one end of the thick branch. It smelled of strong incense and made a layer of smoke. Susan opened the front door to spread the smoke around the door frame.

"I need you to open every door and window in the house; including closet doors and also keep the back door open."

"Should I open the garage door?"

"Yes, please. I'll wait here."

It took over 10 minutes for Melanie to do what was asked. In the meantime, Susan communicated with Marisol and there was a gentle breeze throughout the house. Melanie came back and Susan asked a few questions.

"Is there a grand piano under one of those sheets in the living room?"

"Yes, there is."

"Marisol wants you to uncover it right away. She misses playing the piano."

"Alright."

Susan was almost done when she asked Melanie about Butch.

"Marisol is asking about Butch. Is he someone you work with?"

"Are you kidding me? I haven't met him yet but he will be working at my restaurant. I can't believe you know about him."

"It's Marisol that's asking. She says that he is a good man and deserves a second chance at life. He won't cause any harm."

"That's good to know."

Susan was finished with the sage and took the sea salt out of her bag and poured it in all of the exterior doorways and windows.

"What is the salt for?"

"It keeps the evil spirits out and the good spirits in. There will be no need for an alarm system. Marisol will take care of the house. She wants a dog. Nothing too small."

"Sounds good," Melanie said with a smile.

"I'm finished here. I'll be going."

"How much do I owe you?"

"$175."

"That's it? Here's $250 for your troubles."

"Thank you, and congratulations on your home."

Melanie spent the next two hours unpacking before going back to Paradise Café.

Bruno sat in his kitchen in his usual slacks and polo shirt returning emails on his laptop.

"I didn't know you were taking the day off," said Samantha as she brought in the groceries.

I'm leaving in a little while. Butch will be coming out today and spending time by the pool. He needs some sun."

Samantha got nervous. "What is he, a plant? What am I supposed to do?"

"Nothing. Give him space. He's been living on sandwiches for a couple of weeks and deserves a hot meal. He can warm up the leftover lasagna."

"I'll do that for him."

"Thanks love. I need to get going."

Bruno kissed her goodbye and she finished his glass of wine and took her magazine to the living room. She sat on the fainting couch in direct sunlight and had a perfect view of the pool. It was like waiting for an animal to come out of hiding. Samantha continued to read and looked up every few minutes to see if Butch was outside. Thirty minutes had gone by when she noticed one of the Feds walk toward the pool house and sit on the bench looking for action. Butch finally came out looking pale and thin and he put his towel on the lawn chair. He looked nothing like the man at the airport. He had lost 20 pounds and his head was shaved completely. He had minor surgery on his neck to give him more of a square jaw. There were five surveillance cameras in the backyard and five in the front yard. Each room in the house had a camera except the bathrooms, and of course, that's where most murders take place. Samantha received a text from Melanie asking her to meet for dinner at Paradise Café and she agreed. Samantha watched Butch swim three laps before coming out of the pool to drink his lemonade and apply sunscreen. He put on his sunglasses and laid on the lawn chair to get a tan as Samantha kept watch and tried to read. She dosed off for 45 minutes until she heard a noise in the kitchen. She thought it might be Butch so she walked slowly to investigate. She stared at him in the kitchen for a few seconds before saying hello.

"Hi, remember me? I'm the flight attendant from the airport."

"I never forget a beautiful face. I'm just warming up some food. I can't remember the last time I had a hot meal."

"I understand. I can make some garlic bread." Samantha kept her distance.

"I don't bite and I don't have any weapons on me. We can be civil to one another. Thank you for opening up your home to me. It means a lot."

"It's part of Bruno's job. It's what he does. I just don't want to be in danger."

"This is the safest house in California. It's crawling with Feds and surveillance cameras. One wrong move on my part and I'm done. Let's start over." Butch held out his hand. "I'm Butch Jones. Nice to meet you."

"I'm Sam Kerry. I work for American Airlines and I'm Bruno's girlfriend."

"I don't know what he's waiting for. He needs to put a ring on it. You're stunning!"

Samantha smiled and got the bread out of the refrigerator. "Thank you. You are very kind."

"You're welcome."

They got to know each other for an hour before Samantha had to leave for Paradise Café.

Samantha parked her car under a palm tree. It was 83 degrees outside and the sun was just starting to go down. She went straight to the bar where Bruno was counting the cash from the drawer.

"Hello, babe. I need to put this money in the safe. I'll be right back." He kissed her on the cheek and the bartender made a martini for her. Melanie came out of the kitchen and took off her apron and sat next to Samantha.

"We should go to our usual table. Come on." Melanie took Samantha's drink for her and walked it over to a quiet table in the corner. A server brought both of them water. Classic music from the 1970's played on the stereo.

"So, how did things go with the medium?"

"Very well. She burned sage throughout the house and poured salt in the doorways and uncovered the piano so Marisol can play it."

"What?!"

"Marisol is a friendly spirit that wants to stay. She will protect the house and she's very happy that I'm there. She's not going anywhere and she said that Butch is a good person."

"Who said that, the ghost or the medium?"

"Susan, the medium."

"This is crazy. Doesn't this bother you?"

"Not at all. I've come to terms with it."

Bruno approached the table with drink in hand.

"Hello ladies. Do you mind if I sit down?"

"Not at all," said Melanie.

"So, did you tell Sam about Marisol living with you? I think it's great. It gives you status."

"I've had status my whole life, thank you. The most bazaar thing happened before I left the house. I looked out my bedroom window and noticed the xyst had been cleaned and trimmed and I haven't called the gardener yet."

"Apparently, Marisol does yard work," said Bruno.

"As long as she doesn't hurt anyone or get jealous when you bring home a lover," said Samantha.

"I haven't thought of that but Susan said that she is not evil and just wants someone to enjoy the home. Who knows, she might not even stick around for very long."

"So, on a different not, I met Butch in our kitchen and we had a nice chat for about an hour. I feel more at ease now."

"That's good because he starts working here tomorrow," said Bruno as he buttered his bread.

"What will he be doing?" asked Samantha.

"He's going to be our new chef," said Melanie.

"We need to introduce him to our circle. We'll have to plan a dinner at our house this weekend," suggested Bruno.

"That sounds great. I'll call Margaret to help me plan," said Samantha as she took a sip of her martini.

The Santa Barbara Times hit Maria's front porch and Juan went out in his robe and slippers to get it. October 2, 2011. It was tied in a clear plastic bag so not to get wet in the rain but there was not a raindrop in sight.

"Honey, are you going anywhere today?" asked Maria.

"No, Billy is coming over in a couple of hours to rehearse."

"I just received a text from Sam to read the front-page news."

'SANTA BARBARA SOCIALITE BOUGHT MARISOL MANSION FOR 10 MILLION'

"Look at that. Mel made the papers," said Juan

"That's a good picture of her. Oh, Sam and Bruno want to get together sometime so we can meet a relative named Butch. He is in town. I don't know all of the details. I need to get to the shop. I'll catch you later."

They quickly kissed and she drove off. Sam was also on her way to the shop to meet Margaret and help with some paperwork. She didn't know that Melanie would already be there to discuss Butch and his first day at Paradise Café.

"I had no idea that I made front-page news. That's a first for me. At least they made me sound good for business," said Melanie.

The ladies talked for 45 minutes before Melanie left for Paradise Café. Margaret and Samantha planned a small party for Butch this weekend. Samantha had to get back to work on Monday so the timing was good.

The October sky was over cast with a chance of showers but the party will be held indoors. Bruno borrowed a chef from Paradise Café to cook Italian/American cuisine in their home and Billy offered to bartend. It will be easy since there are only 10 people including the chef from the club who will be seated as a guest at the table even though he's getting paid. Gary was in town which made it very convenient for Margaret. Most of the time she has to dine solo or pair up with Melanie. Billy's wife was always on the road as a backup singer and he hasn't seen her in over three months. He wouldn't be surprised if he was served with divorce papers. She rarely returns his calls.

All of the friends gathered around the bar in the large Patrelli home while Butch was upstairs getting ready. He picked out nice gray slacks and a lavender dress shirt and smelled of Joop cologne. He came downstairs and everyone became silent except Bruno.

"Well, look who it is. My favorite cousin. Everyone, this is Butch. He'll be staying with us for a few weeks and he's also our new Executive Chef at Paradise Café. He started this week."

Most of them were stunned at the resemblance. Butch shook everyone's hand and gave a nice hug to Melanie. Gary whispered in Margaret's ear.

"This explains all of the security outside."

Margaret smiled and took a sip of her Manhattan. Billy slipped out to the patio to take a call from his wife. Juan raised his glass.

"Welcome to Santa Barbara and our circle of friends. I know you will love it here."

Everyone touched glasses and the chef brought everyone I the den to try his Stuffed Mushrooms with fresh Parmesan. Gary snuck away to the bathroom to Google Butch Jones on his smart phone. He was intrigued and excited at the same time. He knew Bruno in Las Vegas and how he helped people in the Witness Protection Program but wasn't sure if he was still in the business. By the looks of it, he was deeper into it. This house had more security than the club he worked at in Vegas. All it was missing were guard dogs.

Billy came in from outside and poured himself another drink before Melanie approached him at the bar.

"Trouble in paradise?"

"She was supposed to come home next week and now she's not. She'll be touring in Argentina instead. She had the option to have someone fill in for her and she made her choice. This doesn't look good."

"I am so sorry." Melanie squeezed his shoulders. "You deserve better. Come on, let's join the gang for now. You need to get her off you mind."

The mushrooms were a hit and this made the chef very happy.

Gary came out of the bathroom with his cell phone to join Margaret.

"I know what you're doing."

"It was business."

"No, it wasn't. You were looking for Butch on the internet. Well, you're not going to find him so leave it alone. I'm sure his identity has been wiped clean. I'm curious as well but he's Bruno's project and we shouldn't go there."

"Understood. Let's just have a good time. You look beautiful tonight."

"Now you're talking," Margaret smiled. "I believe you are trying to score points with me now," she said while tapping his bottom.

Maria was looking lovely with a yellow chiffon dress and strappy sandals as she approached Melanie.

"Mel, have you thought about a house warming party at the Marisol Mansion? I can help you put it together."

"That's a thought. Finding the time is the tricky part. Next month is Thanksgiving and we're thinking about closing the restaurant that day. We can make it a Thanksgiving party. I'll discuss it with Bruno to make sure we are closed."

Samantha was being quiet this evening. She was thinking about work and how she and Bruno weren't spending that much time together. It was partly her fault with all of the flying she does but she was still feeling neglected. She poured herself another glass of wine and mingled with Juan to talk about his music.

The next morning Samantha got up early and let Bruno sleep in. The fog had rolled in and it was a perfect morning for a walk on the beach by herself. It was 6:30am when she pulled on her pink sweatpants and hoodie and headed out the door waving to a federal officer guarding the property. The sand felt good under her sneakers as she noticed a man walking his Golden Retriever and throwing a tennis ball in the water for the dog to fetch. They waved to each other and she moved on. She noticed a sand castle that was half washed away and sat next to it to think about her past. Samantha and her father used to build sand castles on this very beach many years ago and suddenly she missed her parents. Her life has changed so much and she began to question her relationship with Bruno. Was he the one to spend the rest of her life with? She checked her cell phone for her flight schedule and saw that she was flying across the country with a 2-day layover in Chicago. She could do some shopping there. Suddenly, a sand dollar washed up near her feet. She picked it up and looked at the sky.

"Thank you, Jack. I miss you."

CHAPTER 21

It was October 10, 2011 and the wheels touched down on the slick Chicago O'Hare runway and the 747 taxied to an open ramp. Samantha helped a business man get his laptop out of the overhead compartment while another gentleman accidentally brushed her leg with his hand while retrieving his dropped cell phone.

"Excuse me ma'am. I'm sorry," said the passenger. She smiled and went about her business and chalked it up to flirtation. It was the most physical contact she's had in almost a month.

Samantha arrived at the Hyatt Hotel to check in and change her clothes. Neil happened to step out of the Bar and Grill to get some fresh air outside of the revolving door when he noticed a pair of navy blue pumps and beautiful legs. He slowly looked up and noticed Samantha checking in at the front desk. He never forgot her charming profile and bleach blonde hair. He slowly approached her.

"May I help you with your luggage ma'am?"

Samantha turned to her left and her eyes met Neil's. Her smile could light up a room.

"Neil!! Oh, my God! How are you?"

"I'm doing quite well, thank you. It's good to see you. How long are you in town for?"

"Two days. I'm here for some R&R and then off to New York City."

"I'm off work in 45 minutes. Would you like to grab a drink?"

Samantha looked into his sultry eyes and hesitated.

"That would be nice. It will give me a chance to freshen up. I'll meet you in the bar." She went to the elevator and Neil stared at her until the elevator doors closed. Samantha took his breath away.

Samantha walked into the bar wearing jeans, boots, and a tunic blouse. She noticed Neil wiping down a corner table for them to sit. He looked up and they locked eyes. She was stunning.

"What would you like to drink? Are you hungry?"

"I'll take a glass of Chardonnay, please."

"You bet."

Samantha noticed the wonderful music coming out of the speakers. Andrea Bocelli singing in Italian. Neil brought the wine with olive oil.

"How did you know that I was hungry?"

"You need something to soak up the alcohol." They gazed into each other's eyes for 30 seconds.

"I'm in love with this music. It takes me to a relaxing state of mind and brings me joy." Neil was mesmerized by her beauty.

"Why are you looking at me that way?"

"I'm sorry. You are just too beautiful for words."

Samantha blushed. "What would your fiancé say about that?"

"I don't have a fiancé. She left me to find herself. She went to France to study abroad and didn't say when she would be back."

"I'm sorry. Maybe it's temporary."

"It's not. She gave the ring back."

Samantha put her hand on his and her bracelet sparkled in the candle light.

"When did this happen?"

"Three weeks ago." Neil changed the subject. "I thought we'd do some shop therapy," he said.

"Great idea. We can take our minds off of our troubles."

"You have troubles?"

"A few. We can grab something to eat at the mall."

They talked and laughed for 45 minutes before leaving the hotel bar.

It was a crisp 43 degrees in the windy city and Neil was nice enough to heat the seats of his BMW while driving down the boulevard to the nearest mall.

"Can you believe the leaves are turning already? I love this time of year," said Neil.

"We don't get seasons in California. I can really appreciate this scenery. It's beautiful."

"There is a Chinese place and a sports bar in the mall. The choice is yours. We can shop first to work up an appetite."

Samantha looked at her phone to see if Bruno texted her. There wasn't anything. She texted him instead. '*Going shopping and then a quick dinner. Talk to you tomorrow :)*'

"Do you want to start at JC Penny and work our way down?" asked Neil.

"That sounds good."

"I need new work shoes and cologne. Will you recommend a cologne for me?"

"Yes. Macy's has great cologne for men. We'll go there next."

"So, your man bought you that beautiful bracelet? When is he going to buy you a ring?"

"Wow. You just jump right in with the questions don't you."

"Well, yes. There's no easy way to ask that."

"We haven't been together a year yet. We're going at a slow pace. Ask me that question a year from now."

"Ok. He's a good catch. He has money and gives you security. That's what women want, right?"

Samantha sat down while Neil asked an associate for a size 10.

"Women also want love and affection. We don't want to feel neglected and I've been feeling neglected these past couple of weeks. Bruno's been working on a project that is taking all of his time. When he is done with it, I hope we get back on track."

"I'm sure you will. He's not going to mess that up."

"Are those shoes slip resistant?"

"Yes, they are but they look too casual. I think I'll try the loafers instead."

The loafers went perfect with his black slacks and white dress shirt.

"I'm going to get these."

"Good choice," said Samantha. "So, when do you graduate?"

"Not until May. I already have a job lined up at Chicago PD."

"That's incredible! You're so goal-oriented. I like that."

They made their way over to Macy's to try on different fragrances. The associate asked Neil some questions and gave her opinion. "These three colognes will suit you the best. Do you like them?" she asked. They were Joop, Guess, and Polo.

"I like Joop. Samantha, do you like Joop or should I get Polo?"

"I think Joop suits you better. It's not as rugged."

"You don't think I'm rugged?"

"No. You're preppy and sophisticated."

"Well, there you have it. I'll take the Joop," he said to the associate.

They went over to the Chanel counter and Samantha sprayed two perfumes on a sample card.

"Chanel no. 5 is a classic. Do you like it?" asked Neil.

"Yes, but smell this one." Samantha let him smell Coco Chanel.

"Oh! That smells amazing. Are you getting that one?"

"Yes, I am."

"Ok, just don't wear it around me. It'll drive me crazy and I won't be able to control myself."

"Be serious. I'm too old for you."

"Age is just a number and you're a beautiful person. That's all I'm going to say."

"You better not say any more. You're making me blush. Thank you for the compliment."

"You're welcome."

They finished shopping and went to a Chinese restaurant for dinner. The hostess gave them a corner booth and Samantha made sure their shopping bags were between them so they wouldn't sit too close.

"Are we going to eat with chop sticks, or silver ware?" asked Neil.

"Let's eat with chopsticks. Do you know how?"

"No."

"I'll teach you. It's easy."

They both sipped their wine and talked about their careers until the food arrived. Samantha showed Neil how to use the chop sticks and he learned quickly. Neil smiled the entire meal. He became smitten with Samantha.

"I don't work tomorrow. Do you have plans? I can show you the city and we can take in a museum," suggested Neil.

"Really? I would love that. Let's do it."

This is the happiest Neil has ever been. After dinner he took Samantha back to the hotel and he went home.

Samantha woke up to birds chirping outside her window. She took a sip of water from the glass on the night stand and opened the drapes to admire the river. There was a call from Bruno but she wanted to wait until she was able to Skype.

Neil woke up to the sound of his alarm buzzing and he was ready for his 3-mile jog. He drank a small glass of orange juice and off he went. The road was foggy and damp as he noticed a deer dart into the woods. He noticed the trickling sound of the nearby creek and concentrated on his breathing. Samantha was on his mind. Her smile, her laugh, her scent; it was almost too much for him. Neil was in a Euphoric state.

Samantha wrapped her head in a towel while getting out of the shower. She put her robe on and opened her laptop to Skype with Bruno. She was able to reach him at home.

"Hello love. It's good to see you bright and early. I just got up a few minutes ago," said Bruno.

"I've been up for a little while. There's a two-hour time difference. Have you had your coffee?"

"I'm drinking it now. I'm going to the restaurant in a bit and taking Butch. He can't drive without a license."

"Is he going to get one?"

"Not at the moment. It's too risky. The Mafia can hack the system and track his finger prints. We have to figure something out. Enough shop talk. What are you up to today? Are you going to New York City?"

"I leave tomorrow morning. I'm taking in a museum today and maybe read a book."

There was no mention of Neil. She knew he would be jealous.

"Well, Maria will wait until you get back to plan a party at the Marisol Mansion. When will you be back?"

"It's hard to tell with the weather changing. I'll let you know."

Bruno looked at the screen with a puzzled look.

"I can't wait to see you. We need to spend time together."

"You have a full plate right now with Paradise Café and Butch. I'm glad things are working out for him. He seems like a good man."

"He is. He's fond of both of us. Well, I should get going. Enjoy your day."

"You as well. I love you," said Samantha.

Bruno smiled and logged off without a response. Samantha slammed her laptop shut and turned on the TV and got ready. She applied makeup to her porcelain skin and sprayed Coco Chanel in her cleavage. She couldn't understand Bruno's attitude. Maybe he is preoccupied with his work. Either way, it was unsettling and she couldn't wait to see Neil. Neil texted her.

'Good morning beautiful. If you are awake, give me a call.' -Neil

Samantha smiled in the mirror and took a sip of her coffee and called Neil. They agreed to meet in the lobby in 45 minutes.

The elevator door opened to the lobby and Samantha sat on the black and vinyl bench and waited for Neil. She was wearing a light orange pullover sweater, black jeans, black boots, and an ivory scarf. She checked her phone for emails before Neil pulled up and got out of the car and opened the lobby door for Samantha.

"Hey pretty lady. Do you need a ride somewhere?" Neil asked with a big grin. She admired his humor and met him at the door. He was wearing black jeans and a gray argyle sweater. He kissed her cheek and opened the car door for her.

"You look festive and you are wearing Chanel perfume. I can smell it."

"And you are wearing Joop so we are both guilty."

"I hope you're hungry. There is a nice café that serves brunch next to the museum."

"This city is so big and beautiful. I need to visit more often."

"That would be nice."

Samantha admired the sky scrapers as Neil squeezed her left knee and then put his hand back on the steering wheel. Samantha didn't mind and she didn't miss Bruno either. She felt so free.

Neil and Samantha arrived at the parking garage of the 2-story museum and Neil parked the car near the revolving door to the lobby.

"We're going to cut through here to get to the café. We need to take the elevator." Neil held Samantha's hand in the elevator.

"You shouldn't be holding my hand."

"Why not? It's soft."

Samantha smiled. "I have a boyfriend."

"That's right. I keep forgetting."

They continued to hold hands while approaching the café.

"It smells like bacon. I love it. What a cute place!" Samantha said with a smile.

They sat next to the fountain and the server brought them coffee. Samantha spoke a lot about California and how her best friend just bought a haunted mansion. Neil was intrigued and couldn't take his eyes off of her.

Forty-five minutes later, they walked to the museum. It was donation only so Samantha put a twenty-dollar bill in the plastic well. There was a security guard in every room to guard the expensive paintings. Each artist had their own gallery. Samantha noticed a Spanish painting that looked familiar. It was very similar to the one in Mel's mansion. She read the artist's name. *RICARDO SANCHEZ.* She couldn't believe it.

"Neil, this is a Sanchez painting. My friend has one similar to this in her home."

"Wow! Very sultry. I can't believe your friend bought his home."

"I know. I was against it at first but it suits her. She's a glamorous person."

Neil stared at Samantha's profile while she admired the painting.

"I can feel you staring at me. Stop it."

"But, you're a work of art also."

Samantha giggled. "You're so crazy."

They both proceeded outside to the Monet Garden. It was breathtaking. They sat on a bench near a fountain.

"I can't believe you're invited to the Grammy's. It's an honor to attend."

"I know. I feel blessed. I'll have to borrow a gown from my friend, Melanie. I don't have anything to wear."

"Will you send me a picture of the gown that you chose?"

"Of course. She has so many."

"May I kiss your cheek?"

"No."

"May I touch your face?" Neil stroked her cheek and thought about kissing her. They both smiled and walked around some more. The question was never answered.

"We can go to my house and watch a movie if you'd like," suggested Neil.

"Alright but, I have an early flight tomorrow morning to New York."

"I'll have you back before 8pm so you can get a full night's sleep."

"That sounds good."

"I should warn you; I still have photos of my ex around the house."

"You should. It's only been three weeks and she still might call."

"Each passing day, my feelings for her are becoming less and less. I don't see us getting back together."

Neil's home was a fifteen-minute drive from downtown Chicago in an upscale neighborhood. It was a Dutch style home built in the 1980's with high ceilings and diamond-cut glass windows. The front yard was neatly landscaped with stone stairs leading to the large front door. There was a small pool in the backyard. Neil parked his car in the garage and they entered through the laundry room.

"What a beautiful home."

"My parents left it to me. I would never be able to afford something like this on my salary."

Neil showed Samantha around the house. He had a small office to the side that overlooked the garden and a nice painting of his parents above the fireplace. All three bedrooms were upstairs with their own bathroom.

"This home is beautiful."

"Thank you. It's too big. I'm going to rent out a room upstairs to a buddy of mine on the force."

They went into the family room and Neil showed the DVDs to Samantha. They were alphabetized.

"This home is too immaculate. It belongs in a magazine."

"It actually was in a magazine five years ago."

"Where do your parents live now?"

"They passed away two years ago."

"Oh, I'm sorry. What happened?"

"My father had cancer but he went quickly. He didn't know he had it until two weeks before his death. My mother had a heart attack two months later and died in her sleep. She didn't suffer. I believe she died of a broken heart. She loved my dad until the end. They were in their 50's and that's too young to pass away."

Samantha hugged Neil.

"I'm sure that they are proud of your success."

"I think so too. I go into the Police Academy right after graduation next year."

They decided on a romantic comedy. Samantha took her shoes off and cuddled with Neil on the sofa. They nibbled on popcorn and drank sparkling water. She felt comfortable and safe with Neil. They had chemistry. After spending time together, Neil took her back to the hotel.

Samantha woke up to the sound of her alarm and got ready to take the shuttle to the airport. She was sad to be leaving Chicago but knew she'd be back soon. The flight to JFK airport was quick and easy. When she arrived in New York, she called Melanie and asked to borrow a gown for the Grammys even though it was four months away. When Samantha settled into her hotel, she Skyped with Maria and Margaret and discussed plans for Thanksgiving at the Marisol Mansion. Melanie had already hired an interior designer and the house was close to being presentable. Melanie wanted Samantha to stay with her a couple of days so they can catch up on girl time. Samantha texted Bruno and he responded that he was busy at the restaurant and he would call later. She waited for him to call but needed to get some sleep so she could catch her 5am flight back to the West coast.

The 747-jet taxied to the runway as Samantha saw the Statue of Liberty and the Empire State Building in the distance. She thought of Jay for a split second. It felt like a lifetime ago. She thought of Bruno and felt empty and then thought of Neil and smiled. The plane lifted off with the sunrise.

CHAPTER 22

October 11, 2011
Santa Barbara

Samantha woke up Sunday morning and heard splashing in the pool. She looked out the window and saw Bruno and Butch swimming laps and the steam coming off the heated water into the cool air. She went downstairs for coffee and sat on a lounge chair to watch.

"Hello, Love," said Bruno.

"Good morning. Are you going to the Café today?" asked Samantha.

"I'm not sure. Why?"

"I'm going over to Melanie's to discuss the plans for Thanksgiving."

"Alright. Why don't I make you some breakfast before you go?"

"Sounds good. I'll take a shower now."

Maria and Margaret had arrived at the Marisol Mansion for bagels and coffee with Melanie.

"I wanted to sit outside but it's 62 degrees this morning," said Melanie.

"It's nice and cozy inside. I love Sundays. The shop is closed and I can relax and do what I please," said Maria.

"You know I will always hold down the fort if you need a break," said Margaret.

"It's best if I stay busy since Juan is on tour with Billy," said Maria as she spread cream cheese on her bagel.

"Samantha will be here in an hour and there isn't much to discuss about Thanksgiving. Butch will be doing all of the cooking and I think we are having 12 to 15 people," said Melanie as she poured cream into her coffee.

Back at the Patrelli home, Samantha and Bruno were finishing their breakfast.

"Honey, I've been home for three days and we haven't made love or anything. I feel neglected."

"We've been watching TV in bed. Isn't that romantic?" asked Bruno.

"Not really. Maybe tonight we can be intimate."

"I'll be waiting. Excuse me. I have paperwork and payroll to take care of."

Bruno grabbed his laptop, kissed Samantha on the forehead, and went into the office and closed the door.

Samantha pulled up to the Marisol Mansion and she couldn't believe how much was done to the outside. It was bright and cheery just like Melanie. She rang the bell before walking in.

"Wow! This place looks amazing! It doesn't look haunted anymore."

"Trust me, it's still haunted," said Melanie.

Maria poured coffee for Samantha.

"When is Juan coming back home?" asked Samantha.

"Not for another two weeks," answered Maria.

"I'll have to thank him personally for inviting us to The Grammy's."

"No need. You and Bruno are so close to us. We wouldn't have it any other way."

"So, Margaret, when do you see Gary again?" asked Samantha.

"Next weekend. I'm flying to Vegas to see him."

"Exciting!" said Melanie. "Ok, who wants to see my closet?"

"Only if you are getting rid of some clothes," said Margaret with a smile.

"I have some blouses that will fit you."

Melanie noticed that Samantha looked troubled.

"What's going on?" Melanie whispered to Samantha.

"Just some things at home. No big deal."

"We'll talk later."

"Ok."

Ninety minutes went by and Maria and Margaret went to the beach for a walk so Melanie and Samantha were able to talk.

"Will you be off work on Thanksgiving?" asked Melanie.

"Yes, because I worked last year. I'm off on Thanksgiving and Black Friday. I'm probably going to help Maria in her store."

"That's nice of you. I'll be at Paradise Café on Black Friday. So, tell me what's on your mind."

"It's just Bruno. He's been neglecting me lately. He is so preoccupied with the club and Butch…"

"He doesn't mean to neglect you. I'm sure he has a lot going on."

"I've been home for three days and he hasn't even touched me."

"Oh, shit. That doesn't sound like him. He adores you."

"I know. He's too distant. It doesn't make sense. Anyway, I made a new friend in Chicago."

"What do you mean you made a new friend?"

"He's a young man. No big deal."

"You're acting like me now. I thought I was the only one doing that. Who is he?"

"He's a friend. I met him in September and I happened to run into him on my last trip. He's 30 years old or around that age."

"Oh, my God! He's young. Is he a player? Another pilot? Is he married? I don't think it's a good idea to be unfaithful to Bruno. He knows people."

"I'm not cheating. We had dinner and I went to his house to watch a movie. He just went through a break-up. His fiancé left him."

"You went to his fucking house? This is getting interesting. Let's go downstairs and open a bottle of wine."

"His name is Neal and he pays attention to me. He's going into the police academy."

"What's with you and law enforcement?"

"You introduced me to Bruno. I wasn't looking for that type."

"Yes, I remember. You need to talk to Bruno and tell him how you feel. He probably doesn't realize he's neglecting you."

Rose pedals blew in from the open back door and made their way to the Spanish tile. It seems Marisol agrees with Melanie.

The roaring waves hit the sand and the tide brought in more sand dollars than usual. Bruno was coming back from a morning jog and noticed the beautiful round shells. He picked up four of them and realized what a neglectful boyfriend he had become. He brought the sand dollars home and rinsed them off in the kitchen sink and started a pot of coffee while Samantha slept. He cut up some fruit and warmed up some croissants and put everything on a tray to take upstairs to Samantha. He kissed her on the forehead and whispered to her. "I brought you some breakfast. I'm going to take a shower. I'll see you in a few minutes."

Samantha looked at the clock and it was 9:15am. She slept longer than usual and took a sip of water before drinking her coffee. The bathroom was quite large with two sinks, two toilets, a large vanity, a large tub with jets, and a shower with two shower heads and a steam button to be used as a sauna.

Bruno came out of the shower and rubbed Samantha's shoulders. They ended up making love for 45 minutes.

"When do you work again?" asked Bruno.

"I have a short day tomorrow; Las Vegas and back. My long trip is this Friday. I fly to Chicago and then come back on Monday."

"You always end up in Chicago. It's almost like you live there."

The thought crossed her mind as she thought of Neal. Even though things were better with Bruno, she couldn't get Neal out of her mind. She kept an eye on her phone for texts from Neal but he knows better than to text while Samantha was in California. Bruno could easily see it and ask questions.

"You could always fly out with me and meet some of the flight crew."

"Someday. We should plan a trip soon. Our anniversary is coming up."

"What anniversary? I broke up with Jay 10 months ago. To be honest, we're still getting to know one another. I think our one-year anniversary is late February. We don't have an official date."

"Ok, let's make it Super Bowl Sunday."

"of course, I want to spend our anniversary watching football. I need to take a shower and you need to get to work. Goodbye."

Samantha went into the bathroom and slammed the door. She was disgusted with Bruno.

As Samantha cut through TSA at the airport, she thought about Bruno and his back-handed compliments such as making their anniversary on Super Bowl Sunday. Making love to him was a waste of time. She knows they won't be celebrating so she will volunteer to work. Samantha was on her way to Las Vegas and she'll be spending the night at Bellagio Hotel. If she was staying longer, she would have invited Melanie. Samantha texted Neil and said she would like to Facetime tonight and he agreed. This brought a smile to her face. Las Vegas is one of the most romantic cities in the world and she didn't want to spend it alone. She didn't recognize any of the crew members on her flight. It was a rookie flight crew and only a one-hour flight to Vegas.

The plane landed in 90-degree weather and she texted Melanie to see how the plans were coming along for Thanksgiving. Having a dinner party at the mansion was a great idea.

As the shuttle creeped slowly down the strip waiting for pedestrians to cross at dusk, she looked at the hotels and thought about how she had stayed at almost every one of them whether it was business or pleasure. She never thought the Luxor would be a success. It was an odd shape and had a strange odor. Bellagio and The Venetian were her favorites. They were both high-end and classy.

She settled into her room and noticed chocolates on her pillow. She unwrapped them quickly and put two of them in her mouth as though she was hungry. She changed her clothes and went down to the Italian restaurant by the water fountains. There was a water show every hour and the water danced to music. It was a huge attraction and she already had her glass of Chianti and her phone ready to record the show for Neil.

The time was 8pm on a cool rainy evening at the mansion and Melanie and Samantha had picked up sushi for dinner. Melanie had opened a bottle of wine and poured two glasses.

"So, are things better between you and Bruno? You seem more relaxed."

"I try not to think about our problems. Just when things are alright, something odd happens that makes me uncomfortable. For example, we've been dating for 10 months and he wants to make our 1-year anniversary on Super Bowl Sunday. It should be around Christmas time or after the new year. I didn't agree to it and he hasn't brought it up again. He's difficult to talk to."

"Having your anniversary on Super Bowl Sunday is a bad idea. That's in February and you know he'll be in front of the TV all day."

"Exactly."

"Are you still talking with Neil?"

"Yes, we Facetimed in Vegas. I'll be in Chicago this weekend."

"Oh my God. Are you going to see him again?"

Samantha took a sip of wine.

"Yes, that's the plan."

"I hope you know what you're doing."

"I have needs and Neil pays attention to me. He doesn't cut me off and change the subject. He's not selfish like Bruno. I feel like Bruno has sex with me at the right time so I'll stick around. When I drift away, he seduces me. It's a game."

"I suppose you're right. I've seen him do it. He has too much going on to be in a relationship. Think about it. He has the club and Witness Protection. These are both full time jobs."

"Hello! I brought bagels and coffee and I'm ready to help unpack some of these boxes," said Samantha as she put the coffee down. Maria was grateful.

"I'm so glad you stopped by because Margaret is not coming in. She's feeling under the weather today."

"Oh, sorry to hear that. I'll have to call her."

"You're in your uniform so you must be going to work."

"Yes. I have two hours to kill and then I'm off to Chicago for the weekend."

Maria didn't know about Neil and didn't think it was a good idea to mention it. She wasn't sure what the relationship was. Are they friends? Is it a fling? Is it an emotional affair? She didn't want to put a label on it.

"What are you going to do in Chicago? Do you have friends there?"

"I do have a friend there but most of the time I hang out with the crew. I might go to the hockey game." Samantha changed the subject. "It looks like you're up in sales."

"We are and the holidays are right around the corner so everything is in great shape. Are there any Halloween parties I should know about?"

"It's on a Monday but Paradise Café always has a special dinner and a raffle."

"Juan and Billy will be in Vegas so I need to fill my dance card. I'm surprised Melanie isn't planning something since she lives in a haunted mansion."

"I think she'd rather be at the club helping Bruno and Butch," Samantha said.

"There are so many things coming up. Halloween, Thanksgiving, Black Friday, Christmas, New Years, Super Bowl, and finally, The Grammy's."

"Try not to get overwhelmed. I can help with everything. Just breathe and go with the flow. Margaret is a great employee. She does a wonderful job here."

"I know she does. I feel blessed."

Samantha left for the airport and she couldn't wait to see Neil. He was going to pick her up at the hotel and take her to a hockey game.

The plane touched down in Chicago and the shuttle took Samantha to the hotel where she changed into a pull-over sweater and jeans. Neil texted her from the lobby and she took the elevator down. Neil smiled as the elevator doors opened and he saw how beautiful Samantha was. They kissed on the lips and walked outside to the valet. Bruno was the last thing on her mind.

"As soon as we get to the arena, I'm buying you a jersey."

"I won't be able to take it home. How would that look?"

"I'll keep it at my place for future games."

"This is exciting. I've never been to a live game before."

"That's shocking! You've been missing out," said Neil with a surprised grin.

"I hope they have food. I'm starving," said Samantha as she pulled down the visor to look in the mirror.

"We have box seats with a lot of food and drinks. I'll be drinking beer and eating hotdogs but they also have wine and shrimp cocktail."

Neil and Samantha entered the arena and went to the hockey store. There was so much to look at. She picked out a jersey and Neil paid for it. She couldn't believe the cost. She didn't know that jerseys could cost so much. She put it on over her sweater after leaving the store. They went to their box and there were two other couples eating and drinking. They made friends quickly before the National Anthem. Samantha checked her phone to see if Bruno texted. He didn't. After the first period, she went to the restroom to text him and check in. He didn't reply. She figured he was busy and he would get back to her later. Time flew by and the game was over. Chicago won 4-1. This made Neil happy. Samantha couldn't believe how much fun that was. They went back to the hotel and to her room to open a bottle of wine.

"Should we watch a movie?" asked Neil.

"We can if you want."

Samantha changed her clothes into a terry cloth robe. Neil took his shoes and jersey off so he was in jeans and a white t-shirt. They both sat on the bed and scanned the movies to see what they were able to watch. They decided on a romantic comedy and sipped their wine and held hands. Neil couldn't believe how lucky he was to be in Samantha's presence. He looked at her bracelet that Bruno had bought her and wished he could buy her jewelry but that would be crossing boundaries. He already felt awkward being with her in the hotel room. Samantha held her glass and felt comfortable with Neil.

"Are we doing anything tomorrow?" asked Samantha.

"We should take advantage of the spa and indoor pool."

"That sounds fantastic. What time?"

"After a light lunch. Did you bring dressy clothes?"

"No, you didn't tell me to. Why?"

"I'll take you to the mall so I can buy you a dress. I want to take you to Mel's Steak House and they have a dress code."

"Don't you need reservations weeks in advance?"

"I already took care of that. May I ask you something?"

"Sure, what is it?"

"I noticed that you've been looking at your phone. Are you waiting for him to text you?"

"You mean Bruno? Yes. I texted him earlier to check in but I didn't get a response. He gets busy sometimes."

"Well, I hope he gets back to you. You should be a priority."

"I know. I try to be understanding. He has two full time jobs. He's a consultant and runs a restaurant with my best friend."

"He's in law enforcement and so am I. You must have a type."

"My type is someone who is kind and loving and pays attention to me."

Samantha and Neil watched the movie and then Neil went home to sleep.

I was 12 noon the next day when housekeeping knocked on Samantha's door. It woke her up and she opened the door.

"Hi, come on in. I'm glad you knocked or I would have been sleeping all day."

She looked at her phone and Neil had sent a text. He was on his way. She texted back and told him she needed to shower and to wait for her in the lobby. Neil and Samantha met at the buffet 45 minutes later.

"I decided not to wear makeup since we are going swimming."

"You look beautiful either way. I booked a couples massage at 2:30. We can use my discount."

"That sounds lovely." She looked at her phone and there wasn't a text from Bruno. It's just as well. She was having a great time with Neil. "Would you mind if I test my friend, Melanie? It will take just a few seconds. I want to see if she's talked to Bruno."

"Sure, go ahead. I don't mind."

Melanie got back to her right away and didn't understand why Bruno was being so distant. She will ask him how things are going so it won't be obvious that she is prying. He could be losing interest in Samantha.

The server poured Mimosas and coffee and Neil and Samantha proceeded to the buffet.

"What a beautiful spread. I don't want to eat anything too heavy if we are swimming soon," said Samantha.

"I'm glad I get to see you in a swim suit. You have a nice figure."

"Thank you, so do you."

"I like to work out. I need to stay strong."

Samantha could see every muscle and ripple through his tight t-shirt. They enjoyed their breakfast and put their Mimosas in plastic cups and went straight to the pool. The large pool was indoors and had two lanes for swimming laps and the rest for relaxation. The hot tub was in a gazebo setting and looked romantic. They went straight for the hot tub and Neil massaged Samantha's pedicured feet.

"Oh, that feels nice. So, the massage is starting early I see."

"We still have an hour. I might swim a lap or two."

"I would like to also but I had one too many Mimosas and I will be swimming crooked," giggled Samantha.

Neil moved his hand up her inner thigh and she didn't stop him. She knew it was a matter of time before she ended up sleeping with him. Bruno was the last thing on her mind.

Neil got up and went over to the lap pool and took a dive and swam four laps in a row while Samantha looked on. She grinned and couldn't wait to get him upstairs later. She went over to the pool and dove in and only swam one lap.

"I think I'm tipsy so that's all I'm going to do."

Neil grabbed a terry cloth robe and put it around her and they sat on the lounge chairs before going to the spa.

Neil and Samantha checked into the spa and were given cucumber water to sip while getting prepared for the couples massage. The room was dimly lit and smelled of lavender. The music was relaxing with the sound of beach waves in the background. The massage therapists left the room so Neil and Samantha were able to undress on get on their tables. Samantha didn't use the partition in the corner of the room to undress. She quickly took off her robe and swimsuit and hung them on the hook and got under the sheet before Neil had a chance to say anything. He did the same. The two female therapists came into the room and the session began. Samantha immediately fell asleep for 30 minutes until it was time to turn over. She hadn't been this relaxed in years. When the session was over, they put their robes on and carried their swimsuits to the sauna.

"I've never been in one of these. This is fantastic!" said Samantha while holding Neil's hand.

"I hate to ruin a great moment but, may we talk about your boyfriend? Bruno, is it?"

"What about him?"

"He hasn't called or contacted you this weekend. Is everything alright with the two of you? What kind of work has him so busy?"

"Well, I know he should have called by now. He owns a restaurant with my best friend and he's also a consultant with the FBI."

"He should still make time to call you."

"I know."

Samantha pretended not to care and she realized that they were both naked under their robes. She wanted him sexually and didn't feel guilty about it. Her feelings for Neil were so different than the feelings she had for Bruno. Her relationship with Bruno felt more like a job.

The both of them went up to Samantha's room and they made love for the next two hours. She felt feminine; a feeling she has never felt. Bruno never made her feel this sensuous and important. Neil was so much younger and made her feel like a goddess. They held each other until it was time for Neil to leave. He didn't want to over-stay his welcome. He asked the concierge to bring him a single red rose to leave on the nightstand while Samantha slept.

CHAPTER 23

Butch and Melanie were making desserts in the kitchen at Paradise Café while Bruno sat in a booth in the dining room filling out paperwork. Melanie dusted the flour off of her hands and on to her apron and approached Bruno.

"Sam is flying in this morning. Would you like me to pick her up?" aske Melanie.

"I just sent her a text a few minutes ago. I can pick her up."

"She probably didn't get the text. She's in flight right now. She'll get it when she lands. Do the two of you have plans tonight?"

"You've been asking a lot of questions lately."

"She's my best friend and I know the two of you are going through a rough patch. I don't want her getting hurt."

"I don't plan on hurting her."

"I suggest that you make her a priority before you lose her," Melanie said in a firm voice.

"Is that so?"

"Yes. She's the best thing that's ever happened to you so don't fuck this up!"

Melanie went back into the kitchen with tears in her eyes.

"Is everything alright Mel?" asked Butch.

"I need to go home. I'm not well. Will you finish the baking please?"

"I sure will. I hope you feel better."

"I will, thanks."

Melanie got into her convertible and drove with the top down and felt the wind in her hair until she reached the gat of the Marisol Mansion. She pushed the remote to open the gate and drove up the hill.

Maria was at Sand Dollar Jewelers getting the store ready to open. The office window flung open in a gust of wind and her papers blew off of the desk. A white dove appeared in the window sill. Every time something strange happened, she knew it was her brother trying to tell her something.

"Jack?"

The dove flew away towards the hills and Maria shut the window and called Juan.

Melanie arrived at her home to find the white dove on her porch and she heard the grand piano playing in her gallery.

"Marisol? Jack? What's going on?"

She knew it was a spirit and Jack and Marisol were the only ghosts she knew. The white dove flew into the house and landed on the piano and the music immediately stopped. A gust of wind came through the window and blew the drapes inward as Melanie turned with her face glowing in the sun. She gently closed her eyes and took it all in as though she were in a trance.

Samantha was on her flight working First Class when some turbulence started. The captain turned on the 'fasten seat belt sign' and the flight crew returned to their seats. The turbulence became worse.

"This is your captain speaking. I apologize for the rough flight but we have seemed to fly into a pocket of wind. It will be another minute before we can start to descend into Santa Barbara. It is safer to stay at this altitude. I will keep you posted on the arrival. Thank you."

The turbulence continued and there was a very loud cracking noise that Samantha has never heard before in all of her years of flying. Most of the passengers screamed in terror. She looked out the window and noticed the left wing on fire. She immediately got up from her seat and knocked on the cockpit door. The copilot had answered and said the plane had lost an engine.

"The wing is on fire! What can I do?" said Samantha in a panic.

"Get back to your seat and keep the passengers calm."

She looked out the window again and noticed the wing engulfed in flames and now passengers were yelling in fear. The oxygen masks had disbursed from the ceiling as Samantha got on the intercom to make an announcement.

"Please everyone, stay in your seats with your seatbelts fastened. We are having mechanical difficulty and we are almost at our destination. Please stay seated with your oxygen masks on!"

The cabin began to fill with smoke as the plane started to descend and the landing gears were applied. The control tower knew the flight was in trouble and was ready to make an emergency landing. The fire trucks and firefighters were waiting on the runway.

Several long minutes later, the plane became visible to air traffic controllers and they were able to guide the plane but the plane was at an uncontrollable speed to make a proper landing. The tailwind was causing the plane to fly faster. The pilot had to make an executive decision to circle the airport and delay the landing or make a crash landing. Both options were dangerous. Some passengers were unconscious from smoke inhalation and the fire began to spread. There was no choice but to land the plane at an accelerated speed. Breaking News was on every TV channel in town. Bruno noticed the segment on the bar TV at Paradise Café. His eyes grew wide and didn't know if this was Samantha's flight. The plane touched down and spun around twice before hitting the fence. The back of the plane exploded. Passengers were sliding down inflatable ramps and firefighters were assisting the fire. The captain stayed on the plane until every passenger was off. The firefighters continued to hose down the flames. Paramedics assisted victims and the mayor of Santa Barbara showed up to help in any way possible. There was no sign of Samantha. Was she busy helping others or was she caught in the fire? There were 125 passengers on board and not all were accounted for. Bruno got on the phone and started to make calls. He didn't know where to start because he never knew Samantha's flight number. He called Melanie first and then a federal agent to retrieve the manifest. He needed names of all of the flight crew missing or not. His head was spinning and he was sweating through his shirt.

The agent called back with the manifest and he found out Samantha was on board. Melanie called Maria to meet her at Paradise Café. Tears rolled down her cheeks as she drove fast down the hill from the mansion. They met at the bar 15 minutes later and Bruno, Butch, Maria, and Melanie were glued to the TV to see how many casualties there were. So far, only five. Bruno kept calling Samantha's phone and it kept going to voice mail.

"She's not answering," Bruno said in a sad voice.

"She could have lost the phone in all of the rubble; we just don't know," said Melanie. The agent was checking all of the hospitals for injured passengers. There was no sign of Samantha yet.

Ninety minutes and three shots of scotch later, Bruno received a phone call from the agent. Samantha was admitted to Santa Barbara Memorial Hospital in critical condition.

"Let me drive Bruno! You've had too much to drink," demanded Melanie.

All four of them got into Melanie's car and she drove quickly to the hospital. When they arrived at the Emergency Department, Melanie slammed on her breaks and the valet took her car. All four of them ran inside and Maria and Melanie were holding hands and crying. Bruno stepped forward to the nurse's station.

"My girlfriend has been admitted here. Her name is Samantha Kerry."

"I can't discuss the status of the patient. All I can say is, she is in ICU."

"That doesn't sound good," said Maria.

"Are any of you related to the patient?"

"No, we are her family though. We are all she's got!" said Melanie firmly.

Bruno gently pulled Melanie back and suggested they all sit down for a moment while he called the federal agent. The agent showed up five minutes later to see if Samantha had a 'next-of-kin'.

"I'm her emergency contact! It's in her wallet and on her phone," said Melanie anxiously.

"Those items haven't been retrieved from the crash. I will have to pull some strings," said the agent.

"Can you do that? Please?" asked Maria.

The agent went to the nurse's station with the security guard and spoke to the head nurse. The nurse wanted to see Melanie and Bruno together. The nurse took their ID's.

"You must wear these wrist bands before going to the ICU. It's on the fourth floor and the elevator is to your right."

"Thank you, ma'am," said Bruno.

The elevator ride to the fourth floor was the longest ride Melanie had ever taken.

"I hope that she is going to be ok," said Maria to Butch.

"I hear you. I'm going to the chapel to pray," said Butch.

The elevator doors opened to the ICU. Melanie and Bruno stepped out of the elevator and nurses looked as though they were walking and talking in slow motion. Melanie can barely handle the shock that she was in. Bruno proceeded to the nurse's station.

"We are here to see Samantha Kerry," said Bruno.

The nurse scanned both wrist bands. "She is in room 403."

Bruno walked in front of Melanie with his eyes swollen from the alcohol and stress. He thought me might be losing his girlfriend. This was a battle he wasn't ready to face.

"I can't handle this alone. We need to walk in together," said Bruno.

They both walked in holding hands. Samantha was hooked up to an IV and respirator. She had tubes coming out of her nose and mouth and her face was badly bruised. Her right leg was in a cast, her eyes were shut and her head was in a bandage. The doctor walked in with a chart in his hand. Bruno shook his hand and asked questions.

"Doc, what is her prognosis? Is she asleep from all of the medication?" asked Bruno.

"No sir. She just came out of surgery. We repaired her right lung and spleen. Her lung had collapsed and her spleen was injured with internal bleeding. We were able to remove the spleen and stop the bleeding. Samantha had a severe blow to the head and has a brain injury. Her skull is fractured from the impact. Sir, Samantha is in a coma. It's too early to give you any more information."

"Oh, dear God!" said Melanie as she put both hands to her face and wept loudly and rocked back and forward in the chair. Bruno turned completely pale in his face as tears rolled down his cheeks. He was speechless and in shock.

"This can't be happening! We can't lose her! She's my best friend," said Melanie as she grabbed a tissue. She went downstairs to speak with Butch and Maria and left Bruno to be alone with Samantha. Maria cried while Butch held her and then she called Juan and Margaret.

The doctor spoke more with Bruno and gave him encouraging words. "You may visit as long as you like. There is no time limit for comatose patients. We find that they heal faster when loved ones are around." The doctor left the room.

Bruno held Samantha's hand. "Please come back to us. I don't want to lose you. You mean everything to me."

Samantha couldn't respond even if she wanted to. A machine was keeping her alive. If she were to wake up, her life would never be the same. If she were to pass away, Bruno and Melanie will never be the same. This was hell for both of them. Bruno left the room to be with Maria and Butch. Melanie went back into the room to be with

Samantha. She held her hand and stared out the window. The sun was going down and she watched it dip into the ocean. She stared at Samantha's body and watched her chest rise and fall with every breath the respirator was forcing her to take. Her lifeless body was more than Melanie could handle.

To be continued.......

Milton Keynes UK
Ingram Content Group UK Ltd.
UKHW041823031123
431729UK00005B/246